A Stroke
Of Good Luck

A Novel By
Grace Rudolph

PublishAmerica

Baltimore

First printing

ISBN: 1-59286-357-4
PUBLISHED BY PUBLISHAMERICA BOOK
PUBLISHERS
www.publishamerica.com
Baltimore

Printed in the United States of America

This is a work of fiction. Names, characters, and incidents are the products of the author's imagination or are used fictitiously. Any resemblance to events, or to persons, living or dead, is entirely coincidental.

Source: Contemporary Long Term Care Magazine, Learning to Live with the Angel of Death. Vol. 21, No. 5, May, 1998.

ALSO BY GRACE RUDOLPH

PLAYS

Rural Nightmare

Elder's Statements

We're All In This Together

ACKNOWLEDGMENTS

This book is for computer guru Billy Rudolph, Cora Lee Lonardo who made the Plymouth Wax Museum come to life, Matt Muratore, Marylou, Alberta, Debbie, Emily, Daria, and Ted Hardgrove who never lost faith, Elise Nakhnikian, and Loretta Burdette, Laura Hutchison, and Marie Raeder who gave the book a home.

But mostly, this book is for the love of my life, my husband Bill.

"Sometimes not getting what you want is a wonderful stroke of luck."
Dalai Lama

One

I had the dream again last night.

It's always the same dream but each time with a slight twist. It starts with a massive white polar bear. I can see his muscles rippling beneath his fur as he lumbers slowly across a vast expanse of crystal blue ice on four solid paws toward my mother. She turns and smiles at me. His approach is direct and steady as he comes closer and closer.

And then I wake up.

The characters are always the same. There's an unsettling presence behind me that I can't identify but I'm not frightened because my gorgeous daughter Maryanne stands by my side with her arm draped protectively over my shoulder.

Maryanne is six-foot-one and proud of every inch. She has gray eyes like her dad, flawless skin, and short-cropped brown hair tipped with gold - this week. Next week it might be orange. Or blue. She has two earrings in each ear and a discreet navel ring. No nose ring or tattoos, thank God. Maryanne exudes an aura of serenity wherever she goes, diffusing turbulence with her direct gaze and calm, lopsided smile. She never stoops, unlike her five-foot-eight mother.

I still cringe when I remember my-fifth grade Christmas pageant. I was a good head taller than all the other kids, including the boys, so I was cast as Saint Joseph much to the joy of my classmates who took to calling me Joe and sniggering when we passed in the hallways. On opening night I missed my cue as Sister James adjusted my beard and wrenched my shoulders back until they met somewhere in the vicinity of my spine. "Keep your shoulders back, Gloria," she hissed, digging her thumbs into my back. "Stand up straight or you'll wind up with dowager's hump." Ahhh, dowager's hump. If I ever get into serious psychotherapy I'm sure *those* two words will come up a lot.

My older brother James fits the family norm. He's a five-foot-seven middle-aged, sturdy cop now who can instill fear with a glance but when we were children I towered over him. Maybe if my brother Brian hadn't died when he was three I wouldn't be so self-conscious about my height. Brian might have been taller than me. I have always found myself wondering what life would have been like if Brian hadn't died. He was my first brush with death, and guilt.

Maryanne takes after her father's side of the family. Tony Lombardi's my blue-eyed, sandy-haired husband. All of the Lombardis are six-feet tall or taller while my family, the Flynns, are all five-foot-ten or under.

After high school, when I couldn't figure out what I wanted to do other than not go on to college, Mom told me not to worry because someday I'd find a good husband and he would "take care" of me for the rest of my life. Around the time many of my graduating class had found their good husbands and were divorcing them, I was still living with Mom, who had made life very comfortable. The rent was low, the refrigerator was full and we both liked Wheel of Fortune. Then, on a soft spring night in May, Tony Lombardi arrived packaged as a blind date arranged by Mom's best friend, Millie. Tony and his crew had been putting a new roof on her house and, over a glass of iced tea, Millie discovered that he was a gentle, single Catholic who owned his own construction business and in her opinion was "ready to settle down."

Mom loved him. "He's in construction," she said, "you'll never go hungry and he'll be able to fix stuff around the house." This was a not so subtle slam at Dad, who kept a five-pound coffee can filled with rusty 16-penny nails in our dank, cluttered basement beside a tack hammer with a loose head. Dad, an accountant, died of a massive heart attack two years after Brian was found in the pond behind our house.

"Useless," was Mom's assessment of dad. "Useless," she'd declare, as she patched a wall or installed a screen or put in storm windows. She loved Dad and beatified him when he died, but if there's such a thing as reincarnation Mom won't settle for anything less than a tireless carpenter with a passion for a neat, well-lit workbench in a non-obtrusive corner of the basement. Better still, mom will come back *as* that carpenter, with the tool belt and all the trimmings.

When I first met Tony I think she became his champion because he was her last hope for having grandchildren. I was twenty-four and steadfastly single and my brother James, whose wife had been a member of a S.W.A.T. team until they moved into a mobile home on Pine Island, Florida and she became a high school math teacher, informed everyone upfront and frequently that there would be no kids or dogs. The closest thing they had to a pet, besides each other, was a lazy alligator that sunned itself each morning on the concrete boat ramp at the end of their lawn. Besides, she was inclined to root for anyone who might carry me off to a home of my own. Lately, she had been hinting that she wanted the house for herself. But by the end of our first week together when she saw that I had begun to smile and even whistle around the house, she fell in love with him.

In a week's time, Tony had restored something I had lost years ago, on the fall day when I had been left in charge of watching Brian. While Alice Murphy and I tried on each other's Halloween costumes Brian wandered away into the woods behind our house, and by the time we noticed he was gone he was gone forever. Tony had succeeded in opening my heart again to the world around me, which Mom looked on as the First Miracle.

The Second Miracle occurred three weeks later on the evening we decided to elope. "If you're telling me you're eloping," she said, "then that isn't a real elopement, is it? Why not make it official and have a church wedding?" Because we were both older, we explained, we wanted to keep things simple - especially since Tony's sister, Vivian, was having a large wedding in less than a month. Mom's eyes misted over. She insisted they were "tears of joy," but I knew that because her own marriage had been a simple affair she had hoped I would have a large wedding with all the bells and whistles.

After telling Mom, we drove to Tony's parent's home. The plan was for Tony to tell his father about our plans so he could break the news to Ida, Tony's mom, but we arrived to find the house in an uproar. Vivian's fiancé had broken off the engagement because he was having second thoughts, and they had arrived to share *their* news a half hour before we arrived to share *ours*.

"But we sent out the invitations," Ida wailed. Ida would have been at home sashaying down the runway of a Paris fashion house, but this night her honey-colored hair was wisped around her face, curled by the dampness of her tears. As she paced back and forth in front of Vivian and Al, one corner of her gray silk blouse inched free from the waistband of her black linen skirt. The lower pearl button was missing.

"But mama…" Vivian began.

"Don't 'but mama' me, you ingrate!"

"… it's not my fault. Al just doesn't feel ready to get married and settle down yet."

Al put his hand against his chest and looked stunned.

"Don't stand up for that weasel." Ida pulled up short in front of Al, raised her clenched hand and hissed, "After a five-year engagement you're not ready to settle down?" Vivian stepped behind Al. Al's right eyelid twitched. Ida pressed her fist against her mouth, closed her eyes and swayed back and forth until she regained her composure. Somewhat. "We've ordered the cake, the caterer, the limos…" she advanced on the unhappy couple, backing them closer to the doorway, where Tony and I stood.

"Let's not tell her tonight," I whispered to Tony.

"But mama…" Vivian said.

"…the hall, the waiters. Your cousin Vinny got permission from the Cardinal, *The Cardinal*, to perform the ceremony in *your* parish. And the *tuxes!*" She flung her arm out towards her silent husband standing in the corner, "That man, who sacrificed *everything*, money was no object, that man, your father who loves you more than life itself, was willing," her voice became an octave lower and more intense, "that man was willing to sacrifice and put on a tux and give you away and you're throwing it in the garbage can. Shaming this family." She poked her finger into Al's chest to accentuate each word as she said, "You. Are. An. Ingrate."

"But Mrs. Lombardi…" Al said.

"I don't want to hear it."

By now Vivian and Al were standing by our side. Suddenly aware of our presence, Ida shouted at me, "*What!*"

Tony put his arm around me. "Well, that's the bad news, Ma," he said. "The *good* news is that Gloria and *I* are getting married."

Ida's green eyes narrowed. "When?" she said, stalking toward us slowly. The four of us had jammed together in the doorway, making escape impossible.

"Ida," her husband said softly. "Ida." He crossed the room

and touched her shoulder, but she shook him away.

"Stand next to Vivian," she said, eyeing me closely for the first time. I stepped closer to Vivian, who took my hand and held it so tightly I thought I'd sink to the floor and beg for mercy. "How tall are you?" Ida asked as she fluffed up my hair and turned my hands over from side, to side checking out my bitten fingernails.

"Five foot eight."

"We'd only have to take Vivian's dress up four inches."

Tony rolled his eyes and held out his arms toward his Dad, who frowned and turned away to study the watercolor on the wall beside him. Vivian hugged me so tightly I let out a yelp.

"When are you two getting married?" Ida asked.

"We're going to elope, Ma," Tony said.

His mother's mouth formed a determined line as she squinted at me. "You aren't going to put on any weight in the next three weeks, are you?" Frowning, she tugged at the waistband of my jeans.

Tony slipped his arms around Vivian and myself and walked us out the door and down the steps before I could answer. Al followed us to the truck, where Tony held out his arm to stop him and helped Vivian into the back seat. Vivian curled into a ball, clasping her hands on top of her head, and wailed. "Don't waste your tears on him, Viv," Tony said. "He's a no good son of a bitch."

"It's not him," Vivian said, "I just don't know how I'm going to face my friends." Then, under her breath so softly that only I heard her, or *thought* I heard her, she said, "I'm so relieved." She continued to weep as we drove off for pizza and beer and then to the ocean.

Two

The moon was full when we got to Long Beach. We drove the car out on the sand past the summer homes, some with the soft glow of kerosene lamps casting flickering shadows in their windows, until we came to a deserted stretch of beach. The muffled sound of the waves churning pebbles and shells on the shore, along with the sweet fragrance from the long stretch of rosa rugosa on the path, gradually calmed Vivian. Tony and I stretched out on the sand while she splashed through the waves and tossed stones into the water.

"I hope she's okay," I said.

"She's fine. This on-and-off again stuff has been going on for five years. She's a drama queen, but this time things got out of hand." He brushed my hair back behind my ear and pulled me closer, "Wanna call her bluff?" he said as Vivian charged barefoot through clusters of nesting plovers. The small, quick birds retaliated by circling and swooping above her head until they drove her out of their territory and back to us. Vivian sat next to me, pulling her knees up under her chin. By this time I was a little drunk, a new experience for me, but stretched on my back on the hard-packed sand, with a canopy of stars above and a froth of cold surf at my feet I *knew* I could ask the questions that would help Vivian put things in perspective.

"How long have you known Al?" I asked.

"Forever. We were in grade school together but we just got serious five years ago."

"Serious?"

"Yeah. Serious." She added softly, "You know what I mean."

"I know what you mean." I rolled over on my side and looked at her. "Were you happy?"

13

"When?"

"When you were with Al?"

"Are you kidding?" Vivian began counting off on her fingers. "He couldn't keep a job. He was never on time when we were going out. He gambles. He borrows money from me and doesn't pay it back. He says I'm too fat and if I lose weight he says I'm too thin."

I rested my chin in the palm of my hand while the two of us thought that over. Finally, I said, "Why did you stay with him for so long?"

She shrugged. "He got to be a habit."

I rolled over on my back again and looked up at the stars. "Bad habits *can* be broken, Vivian. You can do it."

"You give awfully good advice, Gloria," she said. "I'm glad you're going to marry my brother. It'll be like having a shrink in the family." She stood up and stretched. "For free."

I didn't know it then, but it was the first indication that someday I would become a lightning rod for other people's woes.

Tony told me later that night he thought I did a great job. Although he was glad Al was out of his sister's life, he felt that Vivian's flare for drama would have made his life difficult and the marriage would have been short-lived anyhow. "That's the only reason I didn't deck him tonight. I can see both sides. My sister's got this edge to her that I think a little therapy could help. She could have given Sigmund Freud a run for his money. He would have been so stressed trying to figure her out that he would have switched from cigars to drugs."

"He *did* drugs," I said.

Tony looked at me with new respect.

The next morning Mom told me that while we were at the beach Ida had called. "I love that Ida," Mom said. "She's so down to earth. So easy to talk to." Since her only contact with Tony's mom had been a phone call she pictured Ida as an overweight sweetheart who slogged around the house in floppy slippers and a coffee stained housecoat. "When she found out how disappointed I was that you and Tony were going to be married in some stranger's living room - "

"Mom, what are you talking about?" I said.

"Well, you were going to elope. Right?"

"That's right. We *are* going to elope."

Mom poured me a cup of coffee and we sat at the kitchen table. "Gloria, Ida and I came up with a wonderful plan. You're going to love it." She waited for me to react. I stirred my coffee and waited. "The wedding can still happen," she finally said.

"Who's wedding?"

"Vivian's."

"Vivian doesn't want to - "

"Ida's hemming the wedding gown as we speak. She's coming over this afternoon so you can try it on."

"*What?*"

Mom got up from the table and prepared breakfast. She moved constantly and kept her back to me to avoid eye contact. "I've always regretted that I was never able to put aside money for your wedding."

"Mom. I wouldn't want you to."

"But that had always been my dream," she said. "And do you know what Ida's dream has always been?" I was afraid to ask. "Ida has always dreamed of throwing a lavish wedding. And then, that awful Al - "

"Mom. Where is this leading?"

She came back to the table, sat down and held my hand.

"You're a Catholic. Tony's a Catholic. Your marriage should be blessed in a church."

I looked at my watch and stood up. "I'm going to be late for work," I said.

"Sit down," she said. "We have to talk." Reluctantly, I sat down. "The wedding can still happen," she said. "The only change will be the bride and groom. Instead of Vivian and Al, it will be you and Tony."

"*What*?"

"Hear me out."

"I hope no one's said anything to Tony about this."

"Ida's talking to him this morning. She's also talking to her brother Carmine who's a friend of the Cardinal."

Now it was my turn to hold her hand. "Do you see why we want to elope?" I asked. She shook her head. "Because weddings take on a life of their own and they get out of control. This is a perfect example."

"You're wrong," she said. "This is a perfect example of family love and cooperation."

"What does Vivian think about all this?"

"She thinks it's a great idea. Her bridesmaids are delighted. They're not going to get stuck with dresses they'll never wear."

"Mom, bridesmaids are *always* stuck with dresses they'll never wear."

"But at least they get a chance to wear them once," she said. "And besides, Ida invited a hundred-and-fifty people. She can't call the wedding off. I told her we'd have a short list. Twenty to twenty-five people. Tops. So she's ordering a rush job on those invitations and I'll call everyone on her list."

"And say what?"

She pursed her lips and thought for a moment, snapped her fingers and said, "That there was a printing error. The

16

invitations *should* have read Antonio Lombardi and Gloria Flynn. How's that sound?"

"Nuts."

"Remember when I worked for that collection agency?" I nodded. "The people I called kept their self-esteem, the agency got their money, I got a paycheck - everyone was happy. I can do this."

That afternoon her expertise was put to the test. "*Flynn?*" several of the guests said, "What kind of name is Flynn? Antonio is marrying a *Flynn?*" Several felt this was a perfectly good waste of a good groom.

Three

On the day of the wedding, as we were standing side by side at the foot of the altar, Vinny leaned toward me and whispered, "Gloria, are you sure you want to go through with this? You can say no. It's not too late."

"No?" I said. "No way! I wouldn't miss marrying Tony on a bet."

"Gloria," he tilted his head to one side and gave me a stern, fatherly look. "Are you drunk?"

Tony leaned into the conversation. "Vinny," he whispered, "I can get a woman who isn't drunk. Get on with it."

He did. And we did. And I have never regretted marrying him. His hair is thinner now and flecked with gray and the years of working outdoors have aged him, but he smiles often and has never lost the ability to make me laugh. He's the only person who loves me unconditionally. Other than mom. And Ida. Sometimes I think mom loves him more than she loves me. But that's all right, because I understand her longing for a strong man to depend on. After Dad died, she supported the family by working as a stitcher in a mill. When the mill closed the winter after I graduated from high school, I was working as a secretary in a small ad agency on the Boston waterfront. Convinced I could handle the bills, I tried to talk her into staying home, but Mom was a realist who knew the value of a dollar and had seen my paycheck stub. Every night she pored over the help wanted section of the newspaper, but the only path she could find back into the job market was working for Manpower. Her first "temporary" job stretched into four years of stuffing envelopes for a ruthless collection agency. The collection agency knew it was getting unusually good results from her mailings, although it may never have known about the little notes of encouragement she tucked into the envelopes. On her next job, she Zeroxed lesson plans in the detention offices of a large urban high school filled with surly, combative teenagers. She kept that one for five years. Her next was filing medical charts in a busy doctor's office, a job she loved with a doctor she adored - until he discovered the file system was in total disarray. Everything that began with the letter *M,* mammograms, MRIs, Mrs. Murphy's medical record had gone into one drawer to be sorted out later, when the office was less hectic. Reluctantly the doctor fired her. Mom was good with the big picture but not with details, but she has many other talents.

Although her education ended when she graduated from high school, she continued her piano lessons into her forties and became a marvelous classical pianist. She devours books by Thomas Hardy, does the *New York Times* crossword puzzles in ink, and writes wonderful poems when the spirit moves her. It broke my heart that her last job was bagging groceries at Shaw's supermarket and pushing in long lines of carts from the parking lot in stormy weather.

"You don't need to work," I told her. "Tony and I want to help out. Please. Stay home. Play the piano. Read. Write poetry. Move in with us. For me. For Tony."

"No," she said. "I'm an independent woman." Her reaction was the same whenever we offered to help. Her slight Irish overbite would disappear and her small chin would jut outward as her thin lips became a stern line, her body language for "back off."

For years she stayed put in the drafty three-story top floor apartment in Malden where James and I had grown up. When I found her a ground-floor apartment in Plymouth within walking distance of our home she agreed to let us drive her past the cluster of gray clapboard condos with neatly landscaped lawns and ocean views as gulls cawed and circled overhead. She closed her eyes and took a deep breath of salt air - she refused to go inside. "I might weaken," she said, "and I love my home too much."

That afternoon, after I drove her back to Malden, we stepped out onto the third floor porch, its worn planks tilting precipitously toward the gutter. "Where would I find another place like this, Gloria?" she said, settling into the rusted, squeaking green metal glider. Once, years ago, our cat had fallen off this porch, much to the consternation of the neighbors who happened to be sitting on the first floor porch and caught a fleeting glimpse of orange fur hurtling into the bushes. I was afraid of meeting the same fate if I tried to sit beside Mom. Instead, I pressed my back against the screen door that led to her bedroom and tried to reason with her.

"Mom," I said, "Please come live with us. Maryanne adores you. Bradley thinks you're a wonder."

"Bradley's living in California."

"I know, Mom. But he comes home to visit and once he graduates he'll be moving back home again. He thinks you're the best grandmother in the world." She smiled. "Remember when the children were little and you always took his side when he and Maryanne were arguing."

Mom glanced at me quickly. "I never took sides," she said. "I love *both* my grandchildren. I don't play favorites."

I changed tack, "You could teach Maryanne how to play the piano."

"And leave my nest?" She shook her head. Her 'nest,' was shaded by an arbor of maple trees. From her glider, hidden by the trees, she watched her neighbors' comings and goings without becoming involved in their lives. She had always been a loner, but as her social isolation increased her memory began to fail.

One morning the woman in the downstairs apartment smelled gas. She leaned over her railing and called up to Mom. When there was no answer she went inside and called her on the phone. When Mom still didn't answer she went up stairs and, using the key I had given her in case of emergencies, let herself in to the apartment and found a food-encrusted pan on the gas stove. The pot had boiled over and extinguished the flame. As gas seeped into the apartment Mom slept on the couch. By the time the fire department arrived she was still groggy but able to explain that she had put a pot of Irish oatmeal on the stove, sat down in the living room to finish her crossword puzzle and fell asleep.

I saw the puzzle later. The squares had been filled in with random letters or numbers, or filled in completely. That morning was the beginning of the end of Mom's independence.

Four

My brother James insisted that mom fly down to Florida and stay with them in their mobile home. He sent her pictures of the home, her room, their screened-in Florida porch, his Starcraft cabin cruiser, and an orange tree on their front lawn where she could "pick a fresh orange for breakfast every morning." Reluctantly, Mom agreed to give it a try. What James *didn't* send were pictures of the cone shaped pile of fire ants beneath the tree or the large alligator basking on the boat ramp.

Four months after mom settled in, she felt comfortable enough with the alligator to share a freshly picked morning orange with him. She was startled when the alligator sprang into action with Olympic agility and then horrified when James' wife burst from the house with a blazing Glock and blew the alligator away just before the orange – and Mom's hand – disappeared into its gaping mouth. James called the house that night to tell me they were about to take Mom to the ER at a nearby hospital. "Something's not right, Gloria," he said. "I'd like you to talk to her and see what you think."

"Well, James," I said, "if you'd been attacked by an alligator you'd be a little upset, too."

"That's the whole point. She isn't upset. Not at all."

"Put her on the phone," I said in a voice so filled with rage that Tony looked up over the newspaper he was reading, raised an eyebrow and then ducked behind the paper in mock terror. "What happened, Mom?" I asked.

There was a pause followed by a sigh. Then, she said in a voice she had used when I was a small child and she sat on the side of my bed to reassure me there were no monsters outside the bedroom window, she said, "Well, this afternoon I nearly

22

got eaten by an elephant."

I could hear my exasperated brother in the background, "An alligator, Mom. You nearly got eaten by an alligator."

"Well, whatever it was, James, it doesn't matter because it didn't happen." Her voice was infinitely patient as she put down the phone and apparently crossed the room to reason with James because I could hear their muffled voices in the background. "Mom!" I shouted. "Mom! Pick up the phone. Mom, come back."

Maryanne had padded downstairs and was on her way to the restaurant where she worked as a waitress. She stopped at the doorway to slip on her clogs. "What?" she mouthed to Tony, who shrugged and went back to his paper.

"Your grandmother put down the phone and I can't get her attention, and now she and your Uncle James are arguing," I said, on the verge of frustrated tears. Maryanne dug through her pocketbook and pulled out her car keys, "Damn it! She won't hang up the phone so I can call her back." Maryanne took the phone and blew into the whistle on the end of her key chain. Mom was suddenly back on the phone.

"What going on down there?" I asked. "What's the problem, Mom?"

"What do you mean? There's no problem."

"Well, you know, with the orange and everything."

She lowered her voice and said, "It's not safe here, Gloria. I think the oranges are poisoned, and there's a bad-tempered woman with a gun who lives with James." I could hear that she had cupped her hand over her mouth and the receiver when she whispered, "It's a bad situation."

And that's probably why mom is always part of my dream. We share a genetic knack of getting ourselves into bad situations. In my polar bear dream she's always alone, a

barefooted waif standing on a sea of ice the color of her china
blue eyes. Her short, thick white hair and soft white flannel
nightgown billow gently around her thin body like a drift of
snow, and she's blissfully unaware of the shambling bear
looming larger and larger on the horizon behind her. Even
though Maryanne's at my side, there's a presence behind me
that prevents me from calling out, from reaching Mom. I try. I
fail. I wake up.

But Mom's run-in with the alligator was not a dream, so I
was able to intervene. She had suffered a small stroke, probably
due to her shock at seeing the animal drop dead at her feet, but
the doctor said the side effects were minimal, just a slight
increase in confusion. I suggested she come back up north for
a visit and told her she could have the upstairs bedroom
overlooking the garden behind the house. Although there were
no maple trees, there was a butterfly bush and several
hollyhocks in the corner of the yard. Thank God she never
asked about the apartment in Malden, because it had been
rented to someone else.

If I give the impression of being obsessed with height, guilt,
polar bears, and thanking God then I'm giving you a glimpse
into my soul. Tony says I have all the makings of an obsessive-
compulsive disorder. "You've got OCD, Gloria, and babe
you've got it bad."

Tony knows all the jargon. Four years ago, at his urging, I
went back to school to get my degree in social work. I don't
think I would have graduated if he hadn't enrolled in several of
my evening classes to lend me his moral support. Between the
two of us we would recreate the classes almost word for word
as we drove home together after evening classes. When I knew
I was doomed to fail Anatomy and Physiology after skimming
through *Gray's Anatomy,* Tony found a coloring book that

contained exactly the same information, scaled down and simplified, to help me pass the course.

Five

During spring break of my senior year most of the class had sent out resumes and several of my classmates had jobs lined up. The rest of us had begun to accumulate rejection letters. My friend Apolonia and I agreed to take the licensure test during our last semester so we would be available when the job offers began rolling in.

Apolonia and I had met the first day of class and our friendship had grown over the next four years. She was a self-assured, compact brunette with unruly hair that she captured under woolen caps in winter or battered straw hats in summer. Both of us kept our rejection letters in three-ring binders so that we could compare notes and help each other through the job search.

The week before graduation Apolonia drove me to my interview for case manager with the Department of Social Services. I wanted the job so badly that I was afraid I would seem too desperate, so I asked her to come along to help me keep my angst under control. The small outer office was cluttered with well-used toys and dog-eared children's magazines. A young woman sat behind the receptionist's desk, thumbing through an issue of People while she cradled a phone on her shoulder. She finally looked up and saw us standing there, handed each of us a clipboard with an attached application form, and settled back in her chair with an "uh-huh." Apolonia glanced at the application form and shrugged. "Why not?" I said. "What have you got to lose?"

"Don't worry," Apolonia said. "Working with angry families and distressed kids is not my cup of tea. *You're* the do-gooder who has to save the world one kid at a time. You're a shoo in." She shrugged again. "What the hell."

The next afternoon I found out I had lost the job. To Apolonia.

"Why did you want to work there in the first place?" Tony asked that evening as we stood together at the kitchen sink. I finished drying the dishes and Tony put them back into the cupboard. "You didn't like your internship when you worked with teenagers. They're kids."

"That was different. They were teenagers. I would have been working with little kids. Children."

"Where do you think little kids come from?" he asked, and then answered his own question, "Teenaged girls. You wouldn't have been just working with kids. You would have been working with their non-compliant - "

"Come on, Tony. I'm sick of your lemonade. I lost the damn job and I wanted it. Apolonia's single and just two years older than Maryanne. What does she know about kids! She didn't even want the job."

"I thought she was your friend."

"She is. That's what makes it so terrible. I not only lost the job but I have to cheer her up because she feels terrible because she got it and I didn't. I don't have time to deal with *my* feelings because I'm too busy dealing with *her* feelings."

"Babe," Tony said softly, "I think you wanted that job for all the wrong reasons."

"And what's *that* supposed to mean?" I asked.

"I think you know." We looked at each other for a long moment while I fought back thoughts of Halloween costumes and Brian. "Maybe we'd better drop it," Tony said, putting his arm around me.

Six

The job search wasn't going well. Tony kept reminding me that I hadn't even graduated yet, but that was no consolation when most of my much younger classmates, had managed to find their niches. By the time we met on campus to pick up our caps and gowns half the class had found jobs, and those who hadn't been hired had interviews with agencies that had already rejected me. Everyone seemed sure of what they wanted to do and were certain that it was simply a question of time before they could do it. I had wanted to have a job lined up before Mom's visit but by graduation day I wasn't even sure that I wanted to be a social worker anymore. I began to think the only reason I chose the field was because I knew how to be a mother, and social work seemed like the same job but with benefits and health insurance.

Tony's reassurances and unwavering faith began to annoy me. I could barely conceal the fact that I just wanted to be alone to wallow in my misery and self-pity. I had taken to running on the beach each night after supper, and when Tony offered to come along I'd shrug and say, "That's okay. I'll be back." Eventually he stopped asking, and he and Mom, would be watching the Food Channel by the time I got home with sand in my shoes and salt in my hair, ready for bed after a quick shower and a cup of tea. They had become avid fans of Wolfgang Puck. Mom was convinced Jack Nicholson was down on his luck and had taken on a new personae as a way to make ends meet. "Look how messy he is. A real cook keeps a clean kitchen."

"It's not him. I'm tellin' ya, Mom, that's Wolfgang Puck, not Jack Nicholson."

I would hear them arguing back and forth as I headed up to bed.

I graduated that May. Although I got a 3.9 average, I still felt like a failure – Tony, I told myself, would have gotten a 4.0.

Bradley was flying home from California. He left a message on the answering machine saying he would definitely be home in time for the graduation. As a small child Bradley had always been the one who preferred to play in the back yard or help Tony with chores around the house. Maryanne was more adventuresome. When he decided to accept a scholarship to UCLA instead of a college closer to home we were supportive, but surprised. Bradley was coming home. The family felt complete.

Seven

Maryanne was managing the restaurant where she worked and was getting home later each night.

One afternoon I noticed a bumper sticker on the back of her jeep, 'Sometimes not getting what you want is a wonderful stroke of luck.' "What's the bumper sticker all about?" I asked.

"I thought they were going to make me manager of the restaurant, but the owner's son is coming back and he's going to be taking over. *I'm* supposed to train him because he doesn't have any experience."

"So? What's the bumper sticker got to do with it?"

"I don't know yet. Kevin put it on my car." Kevin was a carpenter who worked for Tony. He had begun dating Maryanne over a year ago but was so quiet I hardly knew him.

"How are things going with Kevin?"

"Fine."

She gave me a smile and drifted off to another room. The conversation was over.

The only thing I really knew about Kevin was that he was as tall as Maryanne, had brown eyes and pulled his shoulder length hair back into a smooth ponytail. Whenever I saw him, he would bob his head and dart a wide, crooked smile in my direction. Maryanne adored him. Tony respected him. Although I found that reassuring, I felt my close relationship with Maryanne had changed since they had begun dating and I began to wonder what kind of a social worker I would be if I couldn't even keep the lines of communication open with my own daughter.

I also began to have nightmares. I dreamed that I was crossing the stage to receive my diploma and looked down to discover I was wearing galoshes with metal snaps that were two sizes too big. The galoshes were unbuckled, and each step was an effort because I was crouching so the hem of my gown would cover the offensive footwear. As I reach out, the president of the college - a tall, frosty woman - pulls back her hand and refuses to hand me my diploma. I am exposed as a fraud, undeserving of academic recognition.

Eight

Rain had been predicted for graduation day, and a large white tent had been set up on the lawn in front of the columned white administration building. But the day was bright and cloudless and lilacs from bushes surrounding a nearby dorm scented the air. We gathered in the student union building, where a continental breakfast had been set up, to put on our caps and gowns. I was too anxious to eat. Several times I checked my shoes to make sure they were the plain black pumps Tony had polished for me that morning and not the galoshes of last night's nightmare.

I didn't know the students sitting on either side of me, but Apolonia, who was further down the row, kept leaning forward to give me a thumbs up and a wink. It wasn't until I heard Maryanne and Bradley hoot, "Way to go, Mom," when my name was called that I was able to locate my family in the crowd sitting on white fold up chairs to my left. When I saw that my mother and my children were standing and saluting me with champagne flutes it suddenly didn't matter that I didn't have a job because the grueling study was over and I had family that loved me. Warmed by that thought I realized Tony wasn't there. The barrier I'd built up against him over the past few weeks felt like an insurmountable wall and I knew I'd miss him if he weren't in my life.

I searched the crowd as I crossed the stage and took my diploma, but I couldn't see Tony until I came off the stage and found him waiting for me with a bouquet of spring flowers. I stepped out of line and into his arms and stayed there, safe and home, until Apolonia tugged at my sleeve and pulled me back into line. "Knock it off, you two," she said. "There are children present."

Nine

That night Mom flew back to Florida. She had decided that she wanted to prove to herself she could survive there. She knew that the gun- toting woman James lived with was his wife and, she told me, she looked forward to "picking a fresh apple for breakfast" each morning. Her condition had been upgraded to intermittent confusion.

Apolonia had invited Maryanne and Bradley to come with me to her graduation party, since Maryanne had gone to high school with several of the people in our graduating class and Bradley knew two of them before going on to UCLA. They drove Mom to the airport before going to Apolonia's. We had planned to meet them there, but after they had left Tony and I had the quiet house to ourselves and I decided to stay home.

After a long shower in the candlelit bathroom I wrapped myself into the rose-colored silk bathrobe Tony had given me for a graduation gift and towel-dried my hair. Tony was in the kitchen when I came out. He had slipped one of my relaxation tapes into the cassette deck on top of the refrigerator and turned off all the lights except one above the counter. He stood at the dimly lit sink mixing martinis.

In the center of the kitchen table was a steno pad, a pen, the telephone book and my three-ring notebook crammed with rejections. Next to the table was the empty kitchen waste-basket.

"What?" I said.

He draped a kitchen towel over his arm, set the martinis on the table, pulled out my chair and tried for a French accent as he said, "Madam, may I join you?"

I dragged the steno pad closer, avoiding the three-ring notebook, the tangible proof I was heading nowhere fast except toward fifty and unemployment.

"Did you find the note?" he asked, pointing to the pocket of my robe.

I reached in and pulled out a small blue envelope. Inside was a sheet of paper on which Tony had written one word: Begin. When I looked up, he had raised his glass for a toast. "Tonight the job search begins. The rest was practice for the real deal."

"No it wasn't, Tony," I said. "The rest *was* the real deal, and I failed." I felt the joy draining away.

"No you didn't," he said, standing up and turning on the overhead light. I squinted against the sudden brightness as he said, "If you really want to get a job you've got to ditch two things: that 'poor me' attitude and these." He opened the three-ring binder and ruffled the pages. "Ditch, em," he said. "Tear 'em up and throw 'em away, babe. That's all past. Tonight you *begin*."

I tore up the first letter slowly and dropped it piece by piece into the wastebasket. It felt good. Then pulled the next two letters free and tore them up. That felt better. I began tearing out fistsful, ripping them up, tossing their confetti into the air and brushing off any that fell on the table or into my lap. "God! That felt good," I said, skimming one off the top of my martini. When the notebook was empty I tossed that into the trash, finished my drink and held the glass out for a refill.

"Not yet." Tony pushed the telephone book closer to me. "We'll start in the yellow pages, with the A's. I'll read. You write. I already looked, the first one's 'abortion.' I don't think you'd want a job in an abortion clinic, or would you?"

"Too dangerous," I said, pulling my chair closer to his so I could look over his shoulder and rest my hand on his thigh.

He looked at me, smiled, then shook his head and said, "Next." He flipped several pages, "How 'bout - "

"Wait a minute, wait a minute. Turn back. Here's one. 'Acting Instruction.'"

"Stay focused." He removed my hand from his leg, licked his thumb and flipped forward a few more pages, "Write this one down," he opened the steno pad and gave me the pen, "Adoption Child and Family Services." I had hardly finished writing down the telephone number when he said, "Adult Care Centers."

"With the elderly? I don't think so. What else have you got?"

"Affirmative Action? A.I.D.S.?"

I shook my head. "I need something upbeat. I'm having a hard time keeping positive right now."

"Okay. That narrows it down, but we'll find you a job that's safe and upbeat. Let's see what we've got in the Bs." He thumbed through a few more pages, read something, shook his head and was about to turn the page.

"What? What is it?"

"Battered Women." We both shook our heads. "Career and Vocational Counseling?"

"I've got to prove *I* can get a job before I go telling *other people* how to get jobs."

"Counseling: Personal and Family?"

"You need at least an MSW for that. I've only got my bachelor's. Am I going to have to get a master's degree before I can get a job?" I dropped my elbows to the table. Tony knew this was a dangerous sign.

"Okay. Okay. Day Care Centers – Adult?"

"No."

"Dentists. Wrong field. Hold on. Electrolysis, Embalmers!" Tony looked up with a grin and seeing I was not amused flipped through the telephone book until we got to the 'Ns' on page 229. The only notation I had made in the notebook so far was

Adoption Child and Family Services. I begged for a drink. Tony bit his lower lip. "I'll make you a drink after you write down the names and telephone numbers of these nursing homes and promise you'll call tomorrow."

"Nursing homes? No, Tony. I'm desperate, but not that desperate."

"You want a job?"

"Welllll…"

"Call 'em."

As he read off the names I scribbled them down, then pushed my glass aside. "What a waste of time and money. What a useless degree. The only job I wanted went to Apolonia - and she didn't even want it."

"Maybe it won't work out for her and then you can apply. Make a deal with her."

"And then what? Wait? For how long?" I wiped the tears from my cheeks with the sleeve of my robe and began to sob, "Can I have another drink?"

"Not tonight, babe, you've had enough," Tony said, "Tomorrow's another day." He put his arm around my shoulder and led me through the house, turning off the lights in each room as we made our way up the stairs to the moonlit shadows of our bedroom. When we got into bed I rolled into his arms and fell asleep immediately.

Ten

The next morning I began calling the names on my list. Tony had written a script for me, which I had changed here and there to make it my own. As each new call met with rejection I became emboldened and began improvising. "I'd like the social service department please."

"Is this a referral?"

After the sixth call, I knew that a "yes" would get me transferred to the admission department or lost in a maze of transfers and hang-ups. On the seventh call – to a nursing home midway down Cape Cod - I said, "No. I'm a social worker." Before I could say anything more the receptionist said, "Could you come in this afternoon for the interview?"

"Well…"

"Around two. Or do you want to come in before lunch? How about eleven?" Before I could answer, she asked where I lived. "It should take you forty-five minutes to drive here," she said. "I'll tell Mr. Hawthorne you'll be here in half an hour." Before I had a chance to ask who Mr. Hawthorne was, she had hung up the phone and I was putting on my make-up, hopping around the bedroom on one leg as I struggled into my pantyhose and adjusting the shoulder pads in the navy blue interviewing suit Apolonia had talked me into putting on my charge card.

Anything seemed possible on that June morning as I crossed the graceful arc of the bridge that spans the Cape Cod Canal. The sunroof was open, and on the radio Frank Sinatra sang *New York, New York* just for me while tankers, tugs and sailboats glided out to sea in the canal below. I knew in my heart I could "make it anywhere" – but not necessarily at Churchill Lakes, the nursing home I was speeding toward. This job interview was just an exercise for the *real* job.

I ran my hand over the smooth leather briefcase on the seat beside me. My graduation gift from Maryanne and Bradley, it made me feel like a professional, not just some new graduate desperate enough to settle for the wrong job. The briefcase contained copies of my resume, a package of back-up nylons, and a well-worn novena booklet to St. Jude that Ida had given me on my wedding day, telling me that on she had, "made a 'flying novena' to St. Jude the night Vivian and Al had called off their wedding. And look how everything turned out," she said.

The wedding had "turned out," all right, and so had our marriage. But the never-ending novena I had begun to St. Jude when I started my job search was enough to rock my faith. When I shared my doubts with Tony he said, "I don't do novenas. I just say, 'God, You lead – I'll follow.' That's it."

When my car was at the crest of the Sagamore Bridge I glanced down at the sparkling water below me and turned up the radio. As Frank Sinatra began crooning *It Was A Very Good Year,* I shouted out at the top of my voice, "God, You lead – I'll follow."

Eleven

I spent close to half an hour doing U-turns in dead-end streets and pulling into and out of driveways. Eventually I began to think I knew where I was because everything looked so familiar. If God was leading, His sense of direction was even worse than mine. I looked at my watch and realized that I was hopelessly late for my interview.

I pulled to the side of a freshly tarred road and tried to calm myself by sorting out my feelings. Had I had deliberately lost my way to avoid the risk of getting a job that I didn't want? The hot morning sun shimmered on the melting tar. In a yard at the end of a near-by street a lawn mower droned, churning up the scent of fresh grass.

I was digging through the glove compartment looking for a street map when I noticed a little boy about six years old, peddling his bike along a dirt path on the side of the road. He was dressed in navy blue Bermuda shorts and a white shirt, and he carried a backpack that kept shifting as he struggled to keep his balance. I called through the open window to him when he reached the car.

He pulled his bike to a stop, straddled it and adjusted his steel-rimmed glasses. "I don't talk to strangers," he said.

"My kids don't either."

He pushed off and pedaled away, staring straight ahead. The backpack shifted dangerously from side to side, throwing him off balance once or twice.

"You passed me four times," he said, when I drove up beside him and slowed the car to his pace.

"I'm lost," I said.

"Yeah?"

As we neared an ivy-covered cottage at the top of the hill, I imagined him dropping his bike when we got there and running to the front door to shout for help. I pictured Tony and Maryanne that evening, sitting in the living room watching television as they waited for me to come home and suddenly recognizing me as the person on the six o'clock news, surrounded by a S.W.A.T. team and a camera crew from *America's Most Wanted.*

"Is Churchill Lakes near here?" I shouted.

"You're not going to ask me to help you find a lost dog, are you?" he said, frowning with the effort of trying to pedal uphill.

"I don't have a dog."

"Or offer me any candy." He shot me a quick sidelong glance.

"No."

"You're not one of those Internet stalkers?"

By now we had reached the edge of the broken down picket fence surrounding the front yard of the cottage. I stopped the car and leaned over to call through the window, "Kid, I had a job interview and I'm late. If you don't know where the damn place is, just say so."

He stopped his bike, hunched over and squinted into the car, "I know what you look like and I can identify you in a lineup."

"Fine. Skip it."

I sat up again and tried to roll up the window but the door was so hot it burned my fingertips. I leaned back, closed my eyes and breathed deeply.

"My great-aunt Rose lives there," he said. "You can follow me but don't get close."

I inched along behind his wobbling bike, past the cottage on the hill, to the end of a shaded tree lined road. A massive beech tree, its gray bark nicked and scrapped in several places, marked the narrow entrance to the nursing home. My tires bumped over its gnarled roots as I pulled into the parking lot. The lush green lawn was divided from the woods surrounding the building by scrub pines and clusters of hemlock trees.

Churchill Lakes, a sprawling one story beige stucco building with a Spanish tile roof, seemed to grow out of the bed of mixed wild flowers, azalea and honeysuckle bushes that surrounded it. Birds fluttered at small plastic feeders attached to several windows.

The little boy pointed to his right and then parked his bike next to a bench beside the front door. He pulled a squalling calico cat out of his backpack and tucked it under his arm, ignoring its pin wheeling legs as he carried it into the building.

I circled the parking lot four times while sweat pooled in my armpits and ran down the inside of my suit, then checked my makeup in the rearview mirror. My mascara was melting, and the half moons beneath my eyes gave me the haunted look of a heroin addict in need of a fix. A horn blared, and I swerved to avoid hitting a car backing out of a parking space. An angry middle-aged woman with short auburn hair shellacked into a helmet blew a cloud of cigarette smoke in my direction. "Okay," she said, "you need it so bad? Enjoy." The tires of her dented black Volkswagen spit up a spray of loose stones that rattled against the front of my car as she drove off. I pulled into the empty space. A sign on the curb read: Reserved-Admissions Director.

The foyer of the building was a large, airy affair with Persian rugs and groupings of wing chairs and sofas arranged around low coffee tables cluttered with National Geographics and Gideon bibles. A heavy chandelier caught the outside sun and scattered rainbows across the room. Two wooden doors with notices and posters taped to their windows separated the foyer from the interior. I fished a tube of lipstick from the bottom of my purse, glossed my lips, and dragged my fingers through my hair.

I was still trying to decide what to do about my mascara when the door beside me opened and a diminutive woman in an electric wheelchair glided into the foyer. The dark roots of her coarse blond hair were noticeable because her hair was pulled up in a tight bun on the top of her head, held in place with a gossamer lilac scarf. Large clip-on faux diamonds sparkled in her earlobes. Her cheeks were rouged, and eye shadow and thick mascara accented her royal blue eyes. Chains of pearls nested on her full bosom. She tilted her head to the side and braced herself on one fist to adjust herself in the chair. "You need a tissue to fix those eyes, honey." She handed me a Kleenex from a box in her lap. "Judy told me someone was coming, but I thought it was the ambulance," she said. "You're here for the job interview, right?"

"How did you know?"

"Power shoulder pads. A dead giveaway."

"Who's Judy? The receptionist?"

She laughed. "Judy's the director of nursing. The *real* power behind the throne," she said. "You have any questions, ask her." She tilted her head and gave me a coy smile. "Or me. I'm Marilyn."

The aroma of coffee and baking bread drifted into the foyer and reminded me I had rushed out of the house without breakfast.

"Come on in." Marilyn waved me inside. A small wooden sign with a silver plaque in the shape of an arrow pointed to a long hallway that stretched out to the right. East Wing. An identical arrow pointed to the left. West Wing. At the far end of each wing was a nurses' station.

"I'll show you where Mr. Hawthorne's office is." Marilyn

curled her finger and I leaned forward. "The word is he's going to walk," she whispered, "and you can take that to the bank."

We paused in the doorway of a sunny room lined with bookshelves and dominated by a large oak table surrounded by comfortable chairs. A woman wearing layered clothing stood in front of one of the shelves, arranging the books. She tugged and patted them into place, then rocked back on her heel, frowned and began again. "That's Elizabeth," Marilyn said. "She's our librarian." Elizabeth turned with a smile and gave me a quick, timid wave before turning back to her work.

As we passed the nurses' station two women, a young brunette and an older redheaded, looked up and smiled, "Meet our new social worker, girls," Marilyn said as we headed towards the elevator. "All the offices are downstairs," she told me as she jabbed the button, "Your room has a window. But don't get excited. You have a view of a storm drain. A frog gets caught in there sometimes but that's about as exciting as it gets." She jabbed the button again.

"I haven't got the job yet." The elevator doors opened.

Marilyn jammed her wheelchair in the doorway and shouted, "She doesn't think she'll get the job."

Maniacal laugher erupted from the direction of the nurse's station, and the redhead's graveled voice called out, "You've got the job, honey, guaranteed."

"That's Ruby," Marilyn said. "You'll love her once you get to know her. It takes time. It takes time." The doors whispered shut and she shook her head, "Sad case. Has a tough life. I wouldn't put up with that rat of a husband of hers. He's a bum. I was married to three losers, but not one of them was a bastard like that one. Beats her up. Gets drunk. He's cracked up two pickup trucks on that tree out front just as you come into the driveway. He's a menace. We've all tried to talk to her, but you can't get anywhere. Maybe you'll have more luck."

We reached the basement and the door slid open. A deeply tanned young woman took me by the arm and pulled me out of the elevator. Her dark hair was pulled into a twist and held in place with a large silver banana clip. Gold bracelets jangled at her wrist. She was wearing a suit identical to mine but I noticed a delicate floral tattoo on her ankle. "It's okay, Marilyn, I've got her. Paul's coming back."

"No! Is he here yet?" Marilyn's eyes glittered.

"They're on their way."

Marilyn fired up the reverse button and her chair rocketed into the elevator cage in nanoseconds, hitting the back wall with such force the doors shuddered as they closed.

"Who's Paul? A friend of hers?"

"Paul's everybody's friend. He coached youth soccer, Pop Warner football, Little League. You name it. He was on the Board of Selectman. Was active in his church. He's a 'frequent flyer.' End stage renal failure." She lowered her voice, "But it's the ambulance drivers that got Marilyn on the elevator."

"I don't get it."

"You will once you've seen them. I'm Judy, by the way," she added. "I'm the director of nursing." She eyed my suit and smiled. "Nice suit," she said. "Did you bring your resume?"

"It's in my briefcase." I turned back towards the elevator, "But I left it in the car."

"That's all right. You can get it later."

The administrator's office was large and cluttered. The walls were hung with framed sports photographs of the young man with spiked blond hair who sat behind the desk, rocking back and forth in a black leather chair. The interviewers were getting younger and younger, and I was feeling older and older

The administrator shot up from his seat. "I'm Buddy

Hawthorne," he said, stretching his arm across the table to shake hands. Piles of papers and a half eaten doughnut fell to the floor. "Sit down, sit down."

I introduced myself as Buddy drummed his pencil against the glass-topped table and he stared at me. I tried to outstare him, waiting for him to blink. Finally he said, "Did you bring your resume?"

Judy put her hand on my arm, anchoring me to the chair. "It's in her car."

"Where was your last job?" he said. I was figuring out how to spin my senior internship with surly teenaged mothers into something marketable when he asked, "When was that? And where?"

"When was what?"

"That last job. When did you leave?"

"It was an internship," I confessed. "It ended shortly before my graduation."

"Perfect! What do you think, Judy?"

"I think you should interview her, Buddy." Judy stood up, "How do you take your coffee?" she asked me.

"Bring me one, too, and see if you can rustle up some more doughnuts," said Buddy, "I had one. What happened to it?" I turned the toe of my shoe so it pointed to the half-eaten doughnut nestled in the pile of papers on the floor beside his foot. He leaned across the desk, clenched his hands so tightly the knuckles whitened, and asked, "How much do you want?"

"For what?" I thought he had forgotten that the doughnut order was in and I was about to be sent on a mission.

"Twenty?" he asked. I tried to figure out how many doughnuts I could buy for twenty dollars. "Okay, twenty-five but that's my top offer."

"Twenty-five?" I noticed my puzzled reflection in the glass

protecting the large photo behind his desk. The photo showed Buddy on a surfboard, wearing denim cutoffs and a toothy grimace. I heard Judy enter the room.

"Okay, okay, thirty but that's *it*," said Buddy.

Judy circled around my chair, gave me a tight smile, and said, "Congratulations."

Buddy pushed the remaining paperwork from his desk to the floor to make room for the tray Judy had brought in. While Judy poured the coffee, he squeezed two doughnuts together and took a bite. "When can you start?" Jelly oozed from the corners of his mouth.

"Monday?" Judy handed me a mug and him a napkin, "Grab your coffee and I'll show you your office." She led me down the hall and into a small, dark, cluttered room. "We'll get a brighter lamp in here," she said.

"What is this?" I pointed to a small black and gold sign on the door. *Director Of Social Services.* "Who's the director?"

"You."

"*Me!*"

"This is your desk. This is your filing cabinet. This is your chair and sofa. You're the Director." She took a chair off the sofa put it on the floor. She pointed to the cluster of folded wheel chairs and walkers stacked in a random heap in the far corner of the room and said, "We'll get these out of here for you, too. What time can you start on Monday? Eight?"

"Wellll…"

"Eight-thirty?"

"You see….."

"Okay, nine. I'll introduce you at morning meeting. We'll put you on the payroll today if you can begin this afternoon and come in over the weekend. Do you have a problem with that?"

"Can I ask a question?"

"Sure. Ask all the questions you want."

"I just graduated in May. How can I be the director of *anything*?"

"Have confidence in yourself. Besides, you're the only one. You're it."

"There's no other social worker," I said, with what I now know would be referred to as a flat affect.

"None."

I sank onto the sofa and she sat down beside me. "I know he seemed a little eager, but we've been without a social worker for two months."

"Why?"

"The last one walked off the job. The one before her walked off, too."

"Why?"

"He harasses people sometimes."

After a long silence while we both thought that over, I tried to stand up, but she grabbed my arm. "Don't worry. Thirty thousand dollars for somebody just out of the chute buys a lot of harassment time. We need a social worker. You need a job. What's the problem?"

"I don't want to work for someone who harasses people."

"If he does, come to me. I'll take care of it."

"I won't know what I'm doing."

"I'll teach you."

"I'll mess up."

"You won't."

After another long silence I decided the only way out of the office was to tell the truth, "I don't want to work in a nursing home," I said.

"Why did you answer the ad?"

"I didn't answer the ad." I dug through my pocketbook for

the shredded Kleenex and dabbed at my eyes and nose. Judy slid one leg over the other and tapped her fingernails on her knee. Waiting. "I always wanted to work with kids. That's why I became a social worker in the first place. When I graduated I applied for a job with the Department of Social Services and my friend, who gave me a ride over, filled out an application blank and *she* got the job. Not me. I should have asked her to wait in the car."

"Why the hell would you want to work for DSS?"

"Because I want to save kids."

"Save kids? Why?"

"Wouldn't you want to save kids?"

"No."

"Find them good homes. Loving parents."

"God, no. Drag kids kicking and screaming away from their parents? People who are trying to beat you up for doing it? Maybe the mother's got a black eye and a baseball bat and the kid's got a pit bull or a rottweiler and they're waiting for you at the top of the stairs, and you can't go alone because you have to bring the cops with you? Who do you think you are? Joan of Arc? What's wrong with you? Look around. This is a nice place."

I looked around the cluttered room, buried my face in my hands, and began to sob.

"This is a good job. Good money, and it's safe," she said.

"Apolonia doesn't even *want* the job. What does she know about kids? She's a kid herself." My sobs turned into an anguished wail, verging on hysteria, "*I* wanted that *job*."

Judy got up to shut the door just as the auburn-haired woman from the parking lot pushed against the door and bustled into the room. She was barely five feet tall, and her massive shoulder pads made her look as wide as she was tall. She sat behind the desk and crossed her feet on top of it. "Aha! I see you've just given her the job description. Is she stayin'?"

"Gloria, this is Maxine Whilerotten, our director of admissions," said Judy. "Maxine, this is Gloria Lombardi, our director of social services. Yes, she's staying." The edge to Judy's voice softened when she said, "At least until she gets the job she wants," she added.

"What job does she want?"

"She wants to work for the Department of Social Services." Maxine guffawed. Judy sat down beside me again, put her arm around my shoulders and leaned her head close to mine. "My sister worked there for ten years before she crashed and burned," she said. Ten years. If Apolonia stayed for ten years I'd be too old to step in when she stepped down. "You don't want to work there. Those people all become hard as nails. You'd have to or you couldn't survive. I can read people and I know you're too tender."

I shrugged off her arm, straightened my shoulders, and plunged the torn, soggy Kleenex to the bottom of my purse. "They've got great benefits. I could get my Masters degree for free."

Maxine dropped her feet to the floor with a thud and jabbed a finger in my direction. "Don't take my parking space ever again and we'll get along fine," she said.

For some reason unknown to me, they both assumed I had decided to stay. Judy withdrew her arm and asked me, "Does this room smell like the bottom of an ashtray to you?" I knew this was a trick question so I tried to make my shrug as non-committal as possible.

"You don't smoke, do you?" Judy asked me.

"No," I said.

"I do," Maxine swaggered to the door, then suddenly turned

toward me. "You got a problem with that?"

"Not at all." I lied. Maxine scared me.

"I'll tell ya something about *her*," she said, pointing at Judy. "She's a nurse that doesn't smoke. That's perverted. Watch your back. Come on," she added. "I'll give ya the two-dollar tour."

Twelve

The rooms were large, and most were homey. Three residents shared some rooms; a few were shared by two. Most of the rooms were filled with homemade afghans, wing chairs, television sets, radios, knickknacks and books. Framed pictures and cards covered the tops of dressers and filled the corkboards fastened to the walls at the foot of each resident's bed. "Short- term residents' rooms are a little stark," Maxine explained. "They're here for rehab and after a few weeks they're buffed up and they go home, so they don't bring in a lotta stuff. Just remember, while they're here their rooms are their homes. Never forget to knock before you go in."

As we passed one of the private rooms she said, "Precautions."

"Precautions?" I asked.

"Yeah. Sometimes ya have to keep 'em isolated, so we have a private room on each wing."

"Why? T.B.? Leprosy?"

She stopped short, dug her fists into her hips and said, "What's wrong with you? Of course not leprosy. Maybe they're gettin' chemo and their white blood count is low and we're afraid they might get sumthin' from *us*." We began walking again. "Or maybe they've just got some disease that's resistant to antibiotics and we don't want to pass it around." She shot me a sidelong glance. "Leprosy!"

I tried to peek into each private room as we walked by. "You're gonna be givin' tours when I'm out at the hospitals screenin' people so pay attention. For example, if you're givin' a tour and you see a UFO in the hall acknowledge it."

"What do you mean?"

"Don't walk by a problem and pretend it's not there, because if *you* saw it *they* saw it. See that?" We were passing a large room filled with round tables, chairs, and an oversized TV. No one was paying attention to the movie on the screen, a black-and-white classic from the forties. Instead, everyone had turned their chairs to focus on a tanned, lanky man in his seventies who was stretched out on a sofa. A small gray-haired woman who looked to be about the same age was cuddled on top of him. He was trying to push her aside and was craning his neck over her head to look in the direction of the television set.

"Hey! Gertie!" Maxine yelled. Several people turned and looked in our direction but the woman on the sofa ignored her. Maxine raised her voice, "*Gertie!*" The woman looked up and grinned. "Take it somewhere else," Maxine said, "Where's your roommate?"

The woman tugged her wig into place, rolled off the elderly man and sat on the edge of the sofa a few minutes to steady herself before standing up. "Playing Bingo," she said.

"Where's your walker?"

"In my room." She helped her friend to his feet and he offered her his arm, "That's where we were going."

"Good idea," Maxine said with a smile. The others in the room turned back to the TV. "That was Bob and Gertie," Maxine said to me. "He's seventy-six and she's eighty-two."

"Eighty-two!"

"Yeah. They had a hot thing going before she came here a year ago. He drives in every day for a visit, usually at lunchtime. The nurse's aides who live around here have all told their kids to stay off the roads from noon to two. He brings in her dog, Jerome. A French poodle. Dumber than dirt. Ya gotta watch 'em. If we ever cut down the beech tree at the front of the drive he'll never find his way out of the parking lot."

I pictured myself unable to find my way out of a parking lot and my eyes began to pool. "What's wrong now?" she asked, "Still fixated on that job you didn't get?" I nodded. "You know what that's called? Job envy. If your friend had wanted this job you'd be pissed off because you couldn't work here."

"I don't think so."

"I know so. I need a smoke." We crossed through a large dining room. The tables had been set for lunch with crisp white tablecloths. In the center of each table stood a small Perrier bottle holding a single rose. Sheer floor-length curtains billowed softly at the open windows. Maxine opened the French doors that led on to a fenced patio filled with heavy-duty white plastic lawn furniture and dark green umbrellas. The patio was surrounded by a raised garden filled with flowers and vegetables. I sat at one of the tables while Maxine kicked off her shoes, stretched out on a recliner and fired up a cigarette. "The reason they hired you," she said, "is they're desperate. The state's comin' and they need a warm body in that office. You're a sacrificial lamb, so to speak. Stick it out until the state leaves and then you can duke it out with your friend if you still want that job."

"Why is the state coming here?"

"They go to every nursing home at least once a year, more often if they find out ya got a problem. They send out a team, usually a couple of nurses, a social worker, maybe a dietician and they nose around for a couple of days to make sure we're taking care of everybody and not killing 'em off or ignorin' 'em. Bottom line: this is the resident's home and the state has a ton of regulations that aren't exactly warm and fuzzy, but they try to make sure everybody's okay." She put her head back and blew out four perfect rings of smoke, "Personally? If I had to come into a nursing home? Off me."

The French doors opened and Ruby, the redheaded nurse,

crossed to one of the plants and pulled off a tomato. She came over to the table where I was sitting and rotated the umbrella in its stand until we were both able to sit in the shade. She offered me a bite of the tomato and when I shook my head she offered me a cigarette from the crushed package she pulled from the pocket of her tunic.

"How's it goin'?" Maxine asked her. Ruby shrugged, inhaled deeply and tilted her head back as she blew out a cloud of smoke.

"Jack's Jack," Ruby's voice was whiskey rough, "He's not gonna change."

Maxine leaned forward and said, "*You* could."

I mouthed the words, should I go? to Maxine. Maxine shook her head and crushed out her cigarette on the floor beside the recliner. "Gloria's our new social worker. Maybe she can help ya. Mind if I ask her?" Ruby shrugged and bit into the tomato. "Gloria," Maxine said, "What would you do if you were married to a guy who came home drunk and beat you up every night…"

"…Not *every* night," Ruby said.

"…Okay, not *every* night," Maxine said, "but if this guy had trouble keepin' a job…"

"…He's had the same job for sixteen years, Maxine."

"Who's tellin' this story? You or me?"

"Well, it's *about* me," Ruby's lips pulled back in what could have been either a smile or a grimace.

Maxine scuffed her feet into her shoes and came over to the table to sit with us. She reached out and squeezed Ruby's hand, "Then you tell 'er, Ruby," she said softly, "Maybe she can help. I'm not buttin' into your life, Ruby, none of us are but we're all worried about you. How many times does he have to run his pickup into the beech tree when he's come to pick you up at night? One of these nights he's gonna kill you. Or himself."

"How many times have we asked them to take down that damn tree?" Ruby said angrily then she sighed, looked over at me and tugged at the sleeve of her tunic to cover the faint purple and yellow marks on her upper arm. "Jack's a nice guy," she said, "when he's not drinking. I used to drink, too."

"Stop defending 'im," Maxine said.

"I'm not defending him. I'm just explaining to her."

"Yeah. Sure," Maxine said.

Ruby took another drag on her cigarette, picked a piece of tobacco off the tip of her tongue and sighed again. "We'll be married twenty-three years this November. I have an investment in this marriage. We have three kids…."

"….who all moved out as soon as they could. Her daughter just moved out last week."

Ruby's eyes filled with tears and she bit her upper lip. "She asked me to move out with her."

"You should have," Maxine said, "Years ago." Ruby stubbed out her cigarette and stood up. "I'm sorry," Maxine said, "Stay. I promise not to butt in again."

"I'm not mad," Ruby said, "It's just no use."

After she had gone back inside Maxine said, "She's taken a restraining order out on him three times. After the state leaves and the pressure's off, work on Ruby would ya?" When I didn't answer Maxine said, "What? Is that a no?"

"I may not be here long enough," I said.

"You just got here. What are you talkin' about?"

"I heard the other social workers left because they were harassed."

"He's a bully. You're a big girl. You can stand up to him. The other social worker didn't give a damn. The one after her was a kid. He'd keep her in his office rantin' and ravin', tellin' her what a lousy job she was doin'–"

"Was she?"

"Nah. He just likes to throw his weight around."

"I'm not going to put up with that."

"Of course not. Just tell, 'im back off. I'm busy. Works for me."

"Okay. I'll stay for a little while until I see how it goes."

"Good for you," Maxine took a deep drag on her cigarette and the smoke poured out of her mouth as she said, "I'm glad to hear you're not gonna let a little harassment stand between you and 30K."

"It won't. Especially if it's true that he's going to be walked out," I said.

She slowly removed her cigarette and her eyes narrowed. Smoke poured from her nostrils. The chirping of a cricket broke the silence between us. "Where'd you hear that?"

"Through the grapevine."

"Here less than a day and you're already on the vine. Not bad. How long you been a social worker?"

"Three weeks."

"You're kiddin', right?"

"No."

She stood up, pinched the ash off the end of her cigarette, licked her fingers, rolled the burnt end shut and dropped it into her pocket. "I'll help ya. So will Judy. We can do this. Go home. Get a good night's rest and I'll see ya tomorrow at nine."

On the way to the front door we passed a darkened room. The shades were drawn. An elderly man in the bed nearest the window was curled into a fetal position with a thin blanket pulled over his head. A younger man, probably in his mid-forties, lay on the bed nearest the door, stretched out on his back with his arms beneath his head. "Paul, can we come in?"

Maxine said. When he nodded we walked to the side of his bed. "How come you're back?" she asked.

"You're the admissions director. You should know," he said without looking at her.

"Somethin' about renal failure, but I don't believe it."

He turned his head on the pillow. Even in the semi-darkness his round face looked bloated and there was a faint dusky cast to his skin. "They said I have six months. Probably less. This time I'm not going home, Max. This is it. I'm here for good."

"Bull," she said, "Who's sayin' that?"

"The doctors."

"Big deal. What do they know?"

"A lot, I hope."

"You're goin' home and this is the woman who's gonna spring ya. She's our new social worker." She turned towards me, "What's your name again?"

"Gloria Lombardi."

He stretched his arms out wide and smiled, "Gloria in excelsis deo. See, Max? The angels have come for me already."

"Suck it up, Cupcake," she said then crossed to the other bed and tugged at the edge of the blanket. A thin, bony hand appeared and the long fingers crept over the hem of the blanket and held it fast. "Hi, Ray," Maxine said, "Wanna meet the new social worker?"

"No." The voice was clear and strong but muffled by the thin blue blanket. Maxine crossed to the window beside the bed and pulled the drape open. Late afternoon sun spilled into the room. "Shut that," the muffled voice said. Maxine looked over at Paul, who nodded. She pulled the drapes shut. "And pull the curtain on your way out." The unseen man in the bed tugged the blanket up further so that it completely covered his head and then withdrew his hand beneath the bedding.

We left the room and headed out the front door and across the parking lot towards my car. "The guy in the cocoon was Ray. Never married. Eighty years old. He's a COF."

"COF? What's that?"

"Crusty Old Fart. Has a brother who has cancer and never visits. Ray swings from totally depressed and completely nonverbal to totally alert and completely sarcastic in a heartbeat. The other guy was Paul," she said. "Single. 30 years old. He's been on the list for a kidney transplant for years." Her breath was coming in short puffs and we slowed our pace. "He's had five admissions to our facility and two to a rehab hospital. His admissions are getting closer together and lasting longer each time, but I've never seen him this depressed. On Monday we'll move Paul to a different room to get him away from Ray."

I slid into the car and buckled my seatbelt. Maxine leaned through the window, "Listen, you're gonna be okay. All ya gotta remember is the Golden Rule. Do unto others, as you'd have 'em do unto you. That's all ya gotta remember and your department will pass the survey with flying colors"

"My *department*! It's just me, Maxine. There's no one else."

"I'm right next door. Pound on the wall if ya got a problem. Go home. Get some sleep and I'll see ya tomorrow morning." She fished several business cards out of her pocket and handed them through the window to me, "Oh, by the way," she said, "do me a favor?"

"Sure."

"On your way home tonight, if you see an accident, throw one of these bad boys on the stretcher, will ya?"

Thirteen

Halfway home it began to rain lightly. I left the window beside me open but closed the sunroof, turned off the radio and enjoyed the hypnotic strum of the wipers against the windshield and the gentle rain on my arm.

When I got home the house was silent. The red light on the answering machine was blinking. I kicked off my heels, changed into blue jeans and one of Tony's shirts, and dried my hair while I listened to the messages. It was comforting to hear Maryanne's voice, if only on an answering machine. She hoped I had a good day and she wanted to hear all about it, but she'd have to wait until tomorrow because she had to work late. The next message was from James. He had a "small problem. Nothing to worry about. Call when you get in." Then, three messages from Apolonia. All short. All asking for callbacks.

By the time Tony got home the rain had stopped. I decided not to tell him about Churchill Lakes until we could sit down and discuss it calmly over dinner. Instead of heating up leftovers Tony suggested we walk down to the waterfront. Maryanne's restaurant was an elegant affair, so we settled for a fish and chips place overlooking the harbor where we gave our order, took a number, and searched for an empty table out on the deck among the crowd of tourists who had just gotten back from a whale watch.

"Maryanne's late again. They should call that place Maryanne's," I said as we waited for our number to be called. "This time he's got her doing the payroll after she finishes hostessing. Last weekend she was their only chef."

"That's not a bad thing," Tony said, "She building up a following."

"Not a bad thing! And who's she building up a following

for? Him? She has no life."

"She and Kevin still see each other."

"When? He works days, she works nights."

"He sees her after she gets out of work."

"How can they keep going on so little sleep?" I asked.

Our number was called. "They're young," Tony said, pushing back his chair and standing up. "They'll be fine. Don't worry about them."

Young. I felt suddenly very old and thinking of working with the elderly wasn't making me feel any younger. By the time Tony returned with our food I was worried about the mortgage, my health, our lack of any real retirement planning, and whether I could find my way back to Churchill Lakes in the morning. "I've settled, Tony," I said. "At this time of life a person shouldn't settle for what they'll be doing for the rest of their life."

"First of all, this isn't the end of your life. This is your first job as a social worker. There'll be others." He squeezed lemon juice onto his fish. "And secondly, thirty thousand a year isn't 'settling.' You going to use that lemon?"

I passed my lemon slice to him and picked at the onion rings on his plate. "Maxine tells me the last four social workers were harassed out of their jobs so they'd leave before it was time for a raise. Is that crazy, or what?"

"If they're using harassment as a form of cost containment, how come you got hired for thirty thousand?" He fished the lemon slice from his glass of iced tea and squeezed it over his fish, "Now *that's* crazy."

He took a swallow of iced tea, and then looked across the rim of the glass at me when I said, "Because he does drugs."

He slowly lowered the glass to the table, tilted his head to the side and gave me a quizzical smile, "Are you sure?" he said.

"Pretty sure."

Tony shifted in his chair and I could see he was uncomfortable.

"Are you going to be safe there?"

"Tony, it's a nursing home. I'm as safe there as sitting on our lawn and watching the grass grow. Besides, there's a rumor that he's going to be fired."

"When his boss finds out how much he paid somebody with no experience I'm sure it'll be more than a rumor."

"Thanks!" I kicked him under the table.

"Whatever, but you've got to admit he sure jump started *your* career. Stick it out for a while, babe, then put it on your resume and move on if you don't like it."

We walked along Town Wharf, past the loud hum of the refrigerated trailers towards a group of fishermen in yellow plastic bibbed overalls and black rubber boots. Bright lights on the dock shone down on the boats tied up to the pier. We stood alongside large blue bins as fishermen in the boats below packed their catches in ice and offloaded them to be stowed inside the trailers.

"I hope Maryanne doesn't marry a fisherman," I said, during the walk home. "That's a hard life."

"She'll probably marry a carpenter."

"Kevin?"

Tony shrugged and put his arm around my waist.

Kevin's truck was parked in front of the house when we got home.

"I thought you had to work tonight," I called up the stairs.

"The restaurant's closed. They had a grease fire in the kitchen," Maryanne called back, "Not my fault. The owner's son dropped out of college and took over as cook." She headed down the stairs, throwing a beach towel over her shoulders, and stopped to slip into her sandals. She was wearing cutoff shorts over her bathing suit.

"Where are you going?" I asked.

"To Long Beach. Kevin's picked up some lobsters and corn."

"Be careful," I said. "Please don't go swimming. It's dark."

"Oh, mom." Maryanne rolled her eyes.

"There are sharks."

"I knew that was coming. Dad, talk to her." She took a bottle of wine out of the cabinet and left the house humming the haunting music from *Jaws*.

After Maryanne left, Tony asked me if she had discussed buying the house three streets over from us. The three-story building was over two hundred years old and vacant long enough for the paint to peel and the window boxes to rot. Several windows were either broken or boarded up and the shutters on the first floor had been torn free. "She and Kevin want to fix it up and reopen it as a bed and breakfast."

"Are they nuts?"

"I already asked them that."

"Have you been by there lately?"

"We met with the realtor and did a walk-through inspection. The basic structure's fine. It's tight. There's a little water damage, but the layout's already there because it was a bed and breakfast before the owners went broke."

"The last owners went broke? That's not a good sign, Tony, not good at all."

"They didn't know what they were doing. I think Maryanne and Kevin do."

"They're kids. Maryanne's twenty-three and Kevin's what…"

"Thirty. And he's a good carpenter, one of my best. He's a

hard worker and he's got a good head on his shoulders. Maryanne could do a lot worse than Kevin." He rumpled my hair and said, "She could marry a fisherman."

I pushed his hand away. "I wanted her to go to college."

"Maybe she will someday. You did. Kevin's got most of the down payment already put aside."

"How did a thirty-year-old carpenter stash away enough to buy an antique house in downtown Plymouth?"

"After his grandfather died two years ago he left Kevin a healthy chunk of money."

"How healthy?"

"Enough. I thought I was going to lose him. But he loves what he does and he's smart enough to do what he loves. I went over the books. We can help Maryanne with her share. She's always wanted to have her own restaurant and every time she's allowed to run a kitchen she builds up a following. This is the perfect opportunity for her. For both of them."

"When did all this happen?" I asked.

"We looked at it this afternoon."

"And when were you going to tell *me*?"

"Tonight. And I'm telling you." I sat down on the couch beside Tony and he put his arm around me and pulled me close.

"How many rooms?"

"Fifteen."

"Oh God. Think of the heating bills."

"Nine of the rooms can be rented out."

"How long has it been on the market?"

"It's been empty for four or five years but it just went on the market today. Kevin knows the realtor, so they were the first ones to see it."

"But Plymouth's a seasonal town. How will they make a go of it?"

"They'll have to figure out how to make their place different. Year- round."

"So they're going to buy this monster together and you're for it," I said, kicking off my shoes and snuggling closer to Tony. "Supposing one or the other of them gets married, what happens then?"

"I think that's why Maryanne wants to put in her share. To keep it a business deal."

"Did she say that?"

Tony became very still, frowned and looked over at me, "By the way your brother called."

"Are you changing the subject?"

Tony splayed his hand against his chest, "No! He said your mom slipped on oranges. I left the message on the machine for you. Didn't you hear it?"

"I heard them. I just didn't want to hear him whine or Apolonia gloat."

Tony handed me the cordless phone. As I waited for James to answer I began to count my worries. I was worried about my job, I was worried about Maryanne, and I was especially worried about why James had called after he began to explain what had happened to mom.

"How did she slip on oranges, James?" I asked.

"One orange. She was out picking an orange for breakfast and there was one that had fallen on the ground and she stepped on it and lost her footing. She fell but she didn't break anything."

"Isn't the orange tree out where the alligator is?"

"Was. He's dead."

"I'm sure he isn't the only alligator in town, James."

There was a long pause and finally James said, "She didn't break a hip."

"A broken wrist is bad enough."

"Don't lay any guilt trips on me, Gloria. Mom's perfectly capable of handling that all by herself."

Tony put his arm around my waist. I leaned my head against his shoulder and held the phone so that he could listen, too. "Put Mom on the phone."

Again there was a long pause. Finally mom said, "If it isn't one thing it's another. Can you believe it, Gloria? Last time it was an alligator; this time it's apples."

"Oranges, mom."

"Apples. Oranges. They're all the same. But I think it's a blessing in disguise."

"How so?"

"Know how I always told you kids that you get the life you need?"

"Ummmm."

"Well, the occupational therapist came to the house yesterday and said I should get back to playing the piano because it would help me get the use of that hand back. I haven't played in years. Not since I moved away from Malden. Where's the piano now?"

"Mom, is this a guilt trip?"

"No. It's a question. Where's my piano?"

Tony leaned close to the phone and said, "Hi, Mom, it's me, Tony. We've got your piano here with us." He raised his eyebrows at me and I nodded, "Why don't you come back North?"

"We miss you," I said. I meant it. "And the piano's going out of tune because there's nobody here to play it."

"Where would I stay? Your house is too small."

Before she could ask us about the apartment in Malden, Tony took the phone and began to pace. When he talked to subcontractors or clients I had seen him pace. I knew he was coming up with a plan. "The porch is huge. Large enough for a bedroom and, if you want, we could even move the piano in there and free up more space in the living room." He listened for a moment and said, "We'll have it tuned." After another longer pause he looked over at me and smiled. "We'll winterize the porch and turn it into a bedroom. Would you like a gas log fireplace out there?" He nodded and handed the phone back to me.

"What do you think, Mom?"

"I think you mean it."

"Are you crying, Mom? Are you okay?" I asked.

"Yes, it's just that Florida is such a dangerous place, Gloria. Now I know why they call it God's Waiting Room. How long do you think this will take?"

"Not long. Maryanne's dating one of Tony's carpenters and he's been trying to get on my good side for a long time."

"When I get back up there I'll check him out and let you know what I think. If he's a keeper Ida and I will come up with a plan. We did all right by you and Tony, didn't we?"

Fourteen

I fell asleep on the couch that night and didn't wake up until Maryanne and Kevin came in at three. When I told them about my call to James and my conversation with Mom Kevin went out to the truck and came back with a tape measure and a pad of paper and began measuring the porch and laying out the bedroom. He even figured out how Mom could have her own entrance to the downstairs bathroom.

"Daddy told me about the bed and breakfast," I said once Maryanne and I were alone in the kitchen and waiting for the coffee to boil. "Are you sure that's what you want to do? That's going to take a lot of hard work."

"I'm sure. Mom, I know Kevin and I can make a success of this."

"How serious are you about Kevin?"

"What's that mean?" I stirred the spoon inside my empty cup until Maryanne reached over, put her hand over mine and forced me to make eye contact. "What's that mean?" she asked again.

"It means that it's risky to go into an expensive financial venture with someone who's probably not going to be in your life forever." The coffeemaker growled softly as the coffee finished brewing.

"So, what's the real question?"

"How serious are you and Kevin?"

"He's nice."

"Nana says she's going to size him up when she moves back and if she likes him she and Ida are going to plan the wedding."

"Oh, Mommm, please!"

"She's probably already asked your grandma to call Uncle Vinny…"

"…Uncle Vinny's not a priest anymore. He's got six kids."

"I don't think that'll stop nana, or grandma." I poured our coffee and set a mug aside for Kevin. "So?" I said.

"'So' what?"

"So how serious?"

"Very serious business partners if we can get the financing. Daddy thinks it's a good buy for us because together Kevin and I have the skills to make it work. You know the house we mean, right?"

"I know the one you mean." I poured our coffee and sat down. "The big monstrosity with the red window boxes. Have you thought out what you're going to do with it if you do get the financing? It's falling apart."

"It just needs a little love." I rolled my eyes and sipped my coffee. "Kevin will give up his apartment," Maryanne said, "and move in while we restore the restaurant and the downstairs rooms. Then we'll work on the outside. Once the restaurant's open and bringing in some income Kevin will close off the upstairs and begin restoring the bedrooms. By next year we should be able to open the second floor as a bed and breakfast while we work on the third floor."

"Sounds like you've been thinking about this for awhile."

"Don't get hurt, Mom," Maryanne said. "We knew you had a lot on your mind and I didn't want to worry you."

"I'm not worried," I lied as I began to stir my spoon inside the empty cup.

Maryanne reached out again and held my hand. "Daddy said he'd help on the weekends. It's going to be a moneymaker, Mom. I can just feel it. I've been working in restaurants since I was in high school," she began counting off on her fingers, "I was a dishwasher, I bussed tables, I was a hostess, I did the ordering and the payroll and managed the books at that small place downtown and I'm a terrific cook. Why should I work for someone else when I can have a restaurant of my own?"

"And, she's got a following," Kevin said when he joined us in the kitchen. I noticed he squeezed Maryanne's knee and she edged her chair a little closer as he spread the plans for the bed and breakfast across the table. I was snared into their excitement and it wasn't until the next day that I realized Maryanne hadn't really answered my question.

"That's 'cause you asked the wrong question," Maxine said, loading up one of the wheelchairs with canes and pushing it out into the hall.

"What question *should* I have asked?"

"'Are you sleeping' with him?'"

"They're not sleeping together."

Maxine was sweating and puffing as she pulled open the first file cabinet drawer and sorted through the jumbled files inside. "How do you know?" she asked, ripping the files up and throwing them into a green trash bag, "Was his hand above her knee?"

"A mother knows."

"Oh, yeah?" Not a hair out of place but she was sweating profusely. Her Red Sox tee shirt and blue jeans clung to her body and there were half moons of sweat beneath her armpits. "Hey, kid!" she suddenly shouted. The little boy I had met on the day of my interview was standing in the doorway. "Go upstairs and get me some more trash bags."

"They asked me to come down and tell you the new admit's here."

Maxine sniffed her armpits and said, "Oh, shit."

"Should I tell them you're not here?"

"No. Tell 'em the director of social services is gonna do the admission." She brought me next door and handed me an inch-thick white mailer. "Have 'em sign everywhere there's a check mark," she said, "Peter Michael will show you where to go."

"Do you still want trash bags?" he asked.

"Yeah," she said, "What are you doin' here today?"

"Granpa and I brought in a new dresser for Aunt Rose. It's white and shiny. I picked out the knobs for the drawers. They're all different colors. It's cool. Wait'll you see it."

"Sounds classy," she said, and then whispered in my ear, "They let him pick out her clothes, too. Wait till you see 'em." She rolled her eyes, waved us towards the elevator and went back to organizing my office while I followed Peter Michael to the nurses' station upstairs.

Ruby looked up over her half glasses and pointed her pen towards East Wing. "Room 201A," she said. "I think we should start screening the families instead of the patients. The daughter would make Attila the Hun look like a walk in the park. Watch out. She's already complaining about the temperature of the room, his roommate, the privacy curtain, the menu, even the ride over from the hospital. The drivers were here and gone in fifteen minutes." She snapped her fingers. "They booked it out of here so fast you would have thought the place was on fire. Poor Marilyn didn't even have a chance to roll over and flirt with them before they were gone. If you go in that room be afraid…be very afraid."

Fifteen

I recognized the room at once. Paul, the young man I had met the day before was gone and Apolonia's dad had taken his place. Apolonia, her hair bristling from beneath a faded blue-and-white bandana, was wearing denim shorts, a tee shirt, athletic socks and hiking boots. She was bent over a suitcase unpacking socks and underwear and cramming them into the two top drawers of the plain oak dresser at the foot of her father's bed. She didn't hear me come in to the room. Ray had emerged from his cocoon of bed linen and was sitting up in bed watching her stack his clothing in piles on the chair in the corner. "The top drawers are mine," he said to me.

"I'll talk to her, Ray."

Apolonia spun around when she heard my voice and rushed over to wrap her arms around me. "Didn't you get my messages?" she asked.

"No," I lied.

"I called six times last night."

"There were only three messages on the machine."

"See? I knew you got them." She sat down on the bed beside her father. "What a stroke of luck. I didn't even know you were here. When did you start?"

"I haven't. Not yet. I begin on Monday. I'm just in today to clean out the office and get myself organized. How long have you been at your new job?"

"A week but it feels like a year."

"Do you like it?"

"No. The first family I met was a living, breathing nightmare. The wife's a battered woman who refuses to leave her husband. The husband's got snakes tattooed all over his arms and shaves his head so everyone can appreciate the devil's head tattoo he's got drilled into the back of his bulging neck. And the *kids*..." Finally, she noticed I was nodding my head towards her father, who was trying to struggle out of bed. She rested her hand on his shoulder and smiled at him, saying, "They're not that bad, dad. The kids are kind of cute." She winked at me. "Let me finish up here and then let's go for a drink." I held out the packet. "What's that?" she asked.

"I have no idea. It's from the admissions director."

She took a pen from her shoulder bag and began skimming the paperwork. "He's too tired to sign all this, aren't you, Dad? I'll sign everything and you just rest." She riffled through the inch thick sheaf of papers and raised her voice a notch. "You remember Gloria, don't you? Remember you met her at the graduation?" Her father summoned up a wan smile and tried to lift his head off the pillow.

He held out his hand, but it fell limply to the bed before I could take it. He gave me an apologetic smile. "I had a heart attack three days ago and I'm so tired all I want to do is sleep," he said, his voice a raspy whisper.

"It's okay, Dad. Sleep."

"Are you going to be all right?" he asked Apolonia. "I'm worried."

"I'll be fine, Dad. Just worry about getting better and I'll be back around suppertime to make sure you get something to eat."

"I'm worried about that guy with the tattoos. Are you going to be safe if I'm not home?"

"I'm going to be fine and you are, too. Rest. I'll sign you in."

"He's got to sign himself in." We both turned. Peter Michael was standing in the doorway. "Unless he's unconscious or crazy he's got to sign himself in."

"Kid, are you a midget?" Apolonia said.

"No, but Attila the Hun was."

Apolonia began scribbling her signature defiantly on page after page, glaring at Peter Michael until he shrugged and disappeared from sight.

"Are you the social worker?" Ray asked.

"Yes." I held out my hand and was about to introduce myself when he cut me short by saying, "Don't bother to tell me your name. You're like all the rest. Here today, gone tomorrow. Social workers change their job like other people change their socks." He tugged the watch off his wrist and handed it to me. "It doesn't work," he said.

"Does it need new batteries?"

"No. I need a new watch." The reflection from the table lamp beside his bed caused a glare that hid his pale blue eyes behind steel-rimmed glasses. When he turned, I noticed that the lenses were flecked with dandruff that had fallen from his bushy eyebrows and the wild crown of white hair that circled his head. "Just like that one."

"I don't know if I can find one *just* like that one."

"Sure you can. It was a graduation gift when I got out of high school." His thin lips disappeared into his mouth when he talked, "You can do it. You're a social worker, aren't ya?"

Sixteen

I took Apolonia downstairs to see my office. As we passed Maxine's office. She was sitting back in her chair with her feet on the desk, smoking a Camel and leafing through a newspaper. Without looking up from her paper, Maxine called out, "Your room's all set. All ya gotta do is move in."

Apolonia stopped in the doorway. "Hello," she said. "Remember me?"

Maxine put down the paper, lowered her feet to the floor, and stubbed out the cigarette in her paperclip dish in one fluid motion. "Of course I do." Her voice was rich and musical, her smile gracious. She glided across the room to Apolonia with both hands outstretched. "I'm sorry I wasn't there when your dad came in today, but I'm helping our new social worker get settled in. Forgive my appearance." She patted her lacquered hair, it moved out slightly from one side of her head and settled back in place when she dropped her hand to her side.

My office impressed Apolonia. The room smelled of lemon oil, and every surface was polished to a high gloss. Two small chairs faced in comfortably towards the couch. Lush ivy spilled over the edges of a planter that had been placed on the windowsill to hide the storm drain. On my desk was a calendar, a pad of paper, three black pens and a yellow highlighter. "Not bad," Apolonia said, running her fingers over the pale yellow-on-yellow print wallpaper.

"What's your office like?" I asked.

"Humph," she snorted, "What office? I've got a cubicle and twenty-three cases."

"Twenty-three cases? There are a hundred and twenty-one residents *here* and I'm the only social worker."

"Each case has at least five very angry people who are all

mad as hell at me, even the ones I haven't met yet, and while I'm trying to do the best for them they're threatening to kill me. Or their families. Or themselves."

"You don't sound happy."

"Would you be? Almost all the kids have ear infections or croup or runny noses. And they throw up in your office. That family I started to tell you about upstairs camped out yesterday for four hours while I waited for the guy from Protective Services to find her a safe house to hide in. Do you know what dirty diapers smell like when you throw them in a wastebasket with old French fries and half-eaten cheeseburgers? One kid, the one with the broken arm, kept rolling a fire engine back and forth over my desk and going "brrooombrooom" forever while his sister crayoned armless stick people on the walls and their baby brother slept in a wash basket on the floor. Did you know babies snore?"

"Yes."

"Well, it was news to me. I've sworn off babies forever. Heck, after meeting this crew I've sworn off kids forever."

"Where was their mother?"

"First she was in the parking lot fighting with *her* mother, then she tracked me down and started fighting with *me,* and when I finally got her into my boss' office *they* started fighting. Her father only agreed to come get her after she told him the tattooed wonder had broken her nose and then he only agreed to come because he thought the guy was still there and he wanted to beat him up with a baseball bat."

"Well, at least she safe. Maybe."

"I don't think so. Once those kids swing into action her dad's going to send her back to her husband and then *I'll* have to go get them."

"How old are these kids?"

"The boy's ten, his sister's eight. I don't remember how old the baby is. Old enough to snore."

"How bad can kids that age be? You're the adult. You should be able to control them."

"Sure, if I was an exorcist. Listen, Gloria, her husband used to stand across the street from the office waiting for the last social worker to come out of work, and then he'd follow her home because she talked his wife into taking the kids to a safe house. She had to get a restraining order against him and when that didn't work she quit. That's why they were in such a rush to hire someone that day." She ducked her head and grinned, "Want my job?"

"When can I start?"

"Are you serious?"

"Yes."

"In about a week and a half."

Seventeen

Apolonia followed me home from Churchill Lake. We parked our cars in the lot across from my house and walked down to the harbor. The Waterfront Festival had been in full swing since early morning but tourists and townies milled through the blocked-off streets and down the road lined with white tents and vendor's stalls. We stopped to buy ice cream cones and let ourselves be nudged along by the slow-moving crowds, wading through groups of small children and ducking balloons, jugglers and clowns. Apolonia stopped to look at jewelry, while I considered buying a stained glass pendant for the kitchen window and instead bought a straw hat. A stage had been set up on the grass at the end of the street, and the sound of a jazz trio floated above the low hum of muted voices and shuffling feet. "Look at this," Apolonia said, going into one stall and holding a dark blue apron up in front of her. The words *Wild Woman* were stenciled in white on the bib of the apron. "This stuff is put out by a group that helps battered women. We've got to buy something here. Got any mace?" she asked the startled woman in charge of the booth, who relaxed once she realized Apolonia was kidding.

I bought an apron for Maryanne and Apolonia bought one for the woman with the broken nose. The scent of brine blew in off whitecaps in the harbor as gusts of wind tumbled discarded food wrappers, confetti, and brightly colored paper ribbons down the street. Thickening clouds scudded across the darkening sky and gulls circled and cawed as people tried to make last-minute purchases while vendors hurried to close their stalls.

"Apolonia," I said, "I know you think I'm crazy but I was serious when I said I'm still interested in that job."

She shivered and said, "So was I."

"What's wrong?" I asked, thinking she had gotten a chill when the wind shifted. "Are you cold?"

"No. I guess someone just walked over my grave." She tried to smile and when that didn't work said, "Gloria, trust me, you wouldn't want this job. You're better off where you are."

Later that night, as I fell into the dream I watched the large white bear lumber toward me across the sea of clear blue ice. I woke with a start just as mother, her white gown billowing around her feet, took her first tentative step onto the ice.

Tony rolled over in bed beside me "Are you okay?"

"Go back to sleep. I'm okay," I said.

"You sure?" he whispered in the darkness.

"I'm sure." But I felt like I was coming down with a strep throat.

Tony rolled over on his side and I moved close behind him and bent my knees against his legs. "I thought I heard you yell 'Apolonia'," he mumbled. "I must have been dreaming."

"You were dreaming," I whispered. "Go back to sleep." I draped my arm over his waist. Unable to find comfort in the gentle rise and fall of his chest, I remained awake until the first rays of morning filtered through the windows and then finally drifted back to a dreamless sleep.

Eighteen

On Sunday morning after breakfast, Tony and I drove past Churchill Lake twice. He drove while I drew a map and jotted down landmarks and mileage. For the first time I was able to relax and enjoy the beauty of the ride, knowing that I would be able to find the place on my own on Monday.

During our first swing through the parking lot, Maxine was getting out of her car. When she looked up at the truck and waved, I slid down in the seat beside Tony and turned my head away.

"What are you doing?" Tony asked.

"Do you think she saw me?"

"Of course she saw you. She waved, didn't she?"

"What will she think?"

"That you can't tear yourself away from the place."

"Go back to the main road and drive by one more time only this time don't go into the parking lot."

We cruised through the side streets and passed Peter Michael on his bike as we neared the front entrance. Peter Michael squinted into the truck and waved. "That's it," I said, "I know where I'm going. Take me home before that kid thinks I'm out to kidnap him again."

On Sunday afternoon Maryanne contacted the realtor, who said he'd meet us at the bed and breakfast. The two of us took the shortcut through the narrow walkway next to the college's granite reference library while Kevin and Tony began closing in the porch and cutting in an entrance to the downstairs bathroom.

The realtor, a large florid blond with a voice so pressured he seemed to be a heart beat away from a massive stroke, rocked from side to side as he walked us through the house, opening doors and closets with the enthusiasm of someone seeing the place for the first time. Tony had been right when he said the place had been empty long enough to become a burden for the current owner. It was a handyman's delight - or nightmare, depending on your outlook.

We followed the realtor as he lumbered up the stairs to the second floor and called back over his shoulder, "The owner's a sweet li'l gal whose dad was in a nursing home for over twelve years." He stopped so abruptly that Maryanne bumped into him and would have lost her footing if I hadn't put my hand out to steady her. "We're talkin' big bucks here," he said out of the corner of his mouth. "He used up all his assets before he died five years ago and now she's dippin' into hers to keep the place from fallin' apart until it's sold."

"Doesn't look like she's doing too good a job," I said. Maryanne gave me a look. "Why didn't she put it on the market right away?"

"Sentimental. Loves the place. Grew up here as a kid. She's livin' in Arizona. Payin' for that place, payin' for this place. She's got a lot of health problems and just wants to unload it."

"I can see why," I said. Maryanne gave me another warning look.

He continued up the stairs, and then stood on the landing while he caught his breath. "Gotta lose weight," he said, shaking his head. "Gotta lose weight." He brushed a handkerchief across his sweating face and pushed it back in his pocket with two fingers. "There's a lien on the place. You knew that, right?"

"A lien," we said in unison.

"Don't panic, ladies. All that means is," he moved his large hands as though he was dealing out cash, "when ya pass papers you'll give us a banker's check for the deposit, and before she gets *her* check they take the money out to cover the lien. It all goes smoothly. I never had a problem in the past and we're not gonna have one now." He started down the narrow hall then stopped, "Ya got a lawyer, right?"

Maryanne surprised me by saying, "Yes."

"Good. You're all set."

As we went from room to room, he explained why the building was in such disrepair. "Once the old guy died she wasn't able to keep the place up. It cost more to keep it open than to shut it down."

"Every time my husband and I walked by this place we wondered why someone would let it just fall apart."

"Ya live near here?" he asked.

"A few blocks away."

"Good. These kids are gonna need all the help they can scrounge up to get this place up and running," he chortled. "Look at that." He reached out and pulled a strip of loose wallpaper away from the wall and dropped it on the floor in one easy swipe. "I had a devil of a time convincing her to board the place up when the windows started getting broken and the dampness began peeling the stuff right off the walls."

"Not *all* the walls," Maryanne said defensively.

He grinned. "Ya love the place, don't ya?" Maryanne nodded.

"Good. I'll tell 'er you're interested." When I nudged Maryanne in the ribs he said, "Don't worry mom, she won't up the price. She wants someone who'll be able to save the place. For these two kids, she might even bring the price down." He picked away a paint chip from the windowsill absentmindedly as he stared out the window. I resisted the urge to beg him not to touch anything else. He stepped back and motioned Maryanne to take his place at the window; "Ya get a good view from here. You can see the harbor if ya look that way, and when ya turn around and look *that* way there's the First Church up there."

"How many fireplaces does it have?" I asked.

"Six."

"Six!"

"Two downstairs, two of the bedrooms up here have 'em and there are two more on the third floor but they're closed up. Last winter someone pried off the boards on the basement window and broke in. Fortunately, the guy across the street saw smoke comin' out of the chimney and he called the cops. That's why the walls around the fireplace downstairs are a little sooty. But your dad said he can fix that up."

"Can we see the top floor?" I asked.

"Ah, lady, you're killin' me." He chuckled and rocked from side to side. "Do ya mind if I wait for ya here?"

"Not at all."

Once we were upstairs and out of earshot Maryanne said, "Mom, if we don't buy this house soon there's not going to be anything left."

"How will you get that musty smell out of the carpets? And it looks like there's an infestation of mice and spiders," I said, pointing to the telltale signs on the floor and in the corners of the room.

We had come into the hallway and were standing at the top of the staircase. "We can do it, Mom," Maryanne said, reaching out her hand and peeling off a sheet of wallpaper. I slapped her hand just as I noticed the realtor's ruddy face looking up at us from the bottom of the stairs, "Look how easy that comes off," he yelled up the stairs. "Ya won't even need to rent a steamer."

Maryanne brushed down a cobweb and stepped on the family of spiders that scuttled across the stained carpet. "We'll paint all the walls white and I'll stencil borders across here," she said, pointing to the edges of the walls. "And look out here." She led me into one of the back rooms and over to a window that overlooked a small back yard with traces of an overgrown garden. "Perfect for a patio," she said. "People can sit out there and enjoy a cocktail while they wait for their table." She raised her finger to her pursed lips and led me into another room, knelt down and lifted the corner of a rug, "hardwood floors," she whispered. "Most of them don't even need sanding."

"How are you going to afford this?" I whispered back.

"Daddy said you could help me out a little, and I've got some money saved up…"

"For college!"

Maryanne sat back on her heels and signed, "Mom, you of all people should understand why I don't want to go to college. Maybe someday down the road I'll go to college, but right now my passion is to have a restaurant of my own. Not everyone has to march to the same drummer. You didn't."

"And look what a hard time I had getting a job."

"But you've got one." When I turned away she stood up and put her arm around my shoulders, "Mom, Kevin and I know what we're doing."

"Have you really given it enough thought?"

"Lots. Dad and Kevin put an addition on the realtor's house last summer, and way back then Kevin asked him to keep an eye out for something we could turn into a bed and breakfast."

"So Daddy knew about this 'way back then'?" Tony and I had always discussed everything involving the children, and I felt this was a breach of trust.

"He knew we were thinking about it. I just don't think he realized how serious we were." She gave me a quick hug and whispered in my ear, "Or he would have told you, mom."

We went back downstairs where the realtor was waiting.

"Ya like it?" he asked me, barring his teeth in a wide grin.

"What's she going to do with the furniture that's still here?" I asked.

"You can make her an offer."

"Most of it's in rough shape."

"Make an offer and if you don't like it, ask her to get it out of here before ya pass papers."

It was impossible not to be caught up in Maryanne's enthusiasm. "Once we pass the papers, mom," she said, "We can get in here and start working. I'll waitress nights and work here days."

"And how about Kevin?"

"He'll give up his apartment and move in so he can work on it evenings and on the weekends, and Dad said some of his guys have volunteered to help. We can do it, Mom," Maryanne said. "This has always been my dream. Haven't you ever had a dream?"

I wanted to say yes, to work with children. Sometimes dreams don't work out. Instead I said, "I hope your dreams come true."

Nineteen

On Monday morning, armed with my map, I left for work a half hour early. As I waited for the elevator Marilyn's electric wheelchair whispered up behind me. She crooked her finger and I bent down. Cupping her hand beside her mouth she whispered, "Today's the day."

"Wish me luck. I hope I can carry this off, Marilyn."

"This isn't about *you*, it's about *him*," she pointed at the floor, indicating the basement offices. "I saw a black Mercedes pull up around seven this morning and two guys from the corporate office got out. They're in his office waiting for him to get here." The elevator door opened, she nudged me with her wheelchair and the two of us got inside. Before the door closed Paul slid in and leaned back against the far wall, bracing himself with a cane. The change in him was remarkable. His complexion was still dusky but his eyes sparkled with a vigor that hadn't been there when I saw him on the day of my interview.

"I'm surprised," I said.

"What? That I'm up and walking?"

"Well, yes. You didn't look good the last time I saw you."

"You didn't look so good yourself," he said.

"What do you mean?"

"You didn't look happy." He laughed. "I've had therapy a few times since the last time you saw me. The Nazi therapist got me." He leaned forward and jabbed the down button with the tip of his cane.

Marilyn glowered at him, "She doesn't like to be called that."

"Sure she does."

"She's Jewish, you dope." The argument was heating up

quickly as the elevator door opened and two men standing in the hallway opposite their elevator looked up sharply from their coffee cups. They were wearing expensive suits and highly polished shoes. "Good morning," they said in unison. Their sudden smiles were too bright. Too forced.

"This is the new social worker," Paul said as we stepped out of the elevator. The older man rocked forward on one foot and took my hand.

"I'm Gloria Lombardi," I said.

He rocked back and the other rocked forward to shake hands and say, "Welcome." After a beat it became apparent they weren't going to introduce themselves or move away from the front of the elevator.

"I'll show you to your office, Gloria," Marilyn called back over her shoulder, "and you can do that intake on Paul."

I raised an eyebrow at Paul, but before I could speak he had taken my arm and was walking me to my office. "What intake?" I asked as I slid behind my desk.

"That was just to get us in here so we can see what's going on," Paul explained. Marilyn positioned her chair so that she could look out the doorway and down the hall. "Don't be so obvious," Paul said to her. Paul seated himself on the couch, scooting from one cushion to another before settling somewhere in the middle. "I can see everything from here if you move, Marilyn."

"I'm just going to go by the office. I'll bet it's cleaned out already."

"If the office is empty they're not going to let him off the elevator."

It turned out that they were both right.

I never saw Buddy again. He hired me, they fired him, and later that afternoon a new administrator moved into his office.

Twenty

After morning meeting and an introduction to the other department heads, Judy brought me back to my office and gave me a cup of coffee, a black pen and a stack of letter sized lined cards. On the top one she had printed:

'Adjustment to new social worker.
Will adjust to new social worker.
One to one visits to develop rapport while
assessing needs.'

"What's this?" I asked.

"It's a care plan. There has to be one for every problem a resident has. The nurses do them. Dietary does one. So does the activities department. This is a good one for your department," Judy said. "And this," she gave me a list of names, "is the daily census. It's the name of every resident in the place as of this morning." I scanned the long list; "By the end of today you've got to write a care plan on one of these sheets for every resident in the place. We're not full, so you only have to write that 121 times. We usually have 123 residents but we're down two beds." I sipped my coffee and frowned at the list.

"Have you ever done this before?" she asked.

"Sure, when I was a kid."

She looked puzzled. "What do you mean?"

"One time I had to stay after school and write 'I will not talk in class' a hundred and fifty times on the blackboard."

Judy folded her hands, leaned across the desk and said in a low, intense voice, "Gloria, please tell me you are kidding about not knowing how to do this job."

"I'm not kidding."

"Gloria, the state's coming. Any day now. You're old enough to look seasoned. If you don't know what you're doing," she shot me a wide-eyed, desperate look, "fake it."

After she left the room and shut the door I checked the back of my hands and decided the freckles were actually age spots. With a sigh, I picked up the pen and got to work.

Around midmorning Maxine brought me another cup of coffee and a Danish and showed me where the blank psychosocial history forms were kept. Paul, who had been in and out of the facility several times, helped me fill out his history. "See?" he said, when we were done, "That wasn't so bad, was it? Feeling better?"

"What do you mean?"

"You're not happy here, are you?"

"No, I like it here," I lied.

"That's okay," he grunted as he leaned on his cane and pushed himself out of the chair, "It'll grow on you, kid."

Before I had a chance to insist that I was happy Ruby took me by the arm and led me down the hall. "You've got to do something," she said.

"What's the problem?"

"Disgruntled roommates. They're both asking for a room change. They do this all the time, but when push-comes-to-shove they back off. Both of them. This time's different. I think you might be able to get one of them to move. If you can carry this off your life will be a whole lot easier." She brought me to a room at the end of the hall. "Jacob," she rapped on the wall beside the open door, "Can we come in?"

"Of course. Of course. Forgive me if I don't stand up." He gently placed the china teacup he was holding on the table beside his upholstered rocker and held out his hand.

"This is Gloria," Ruby said. "She's our new social worker."

The shadows thrown by the floor lamp beside his chair accentuated the sharpness of his cheekbones. "Do you see what

I'm dealing with, Ruby?" he said. With a languid wave of his hand he indicated the other side of the room where a middle-aged man with an enormous belly sat on the edge of a bed holding a TV remote and staring at flickering images on a small black and white television screen. A narrow strip of black tape snaked across the floor and up the wall, dividing the room in half.

"Who put that tape there?" Ruby asked. The man sitting on the edge of the bed shrugged, pointed the remote at the TV. "Sylvester," Ruby said, crossing to his bed, "Who put that tape there?"

He glanced up briefly, and then scrolled through the channels. "I didn't," he said.

I held out my hand and said, "Hello, Sylvester." He ignored me.

"His son put the tape there," Jacob said. Ruby was about to peel it off until Jacob said, "I wouldn't do that. It'll take the wallpaper with it."

"I'll get maintenance up here," Ruby said.

"No. Leave it." Jacob picked up his teacup, "It lends a rustic charm to the room."

"Would you like a different room?" I asked Jacob.

"I'd like *him* to have a different room," Jacob said.

"I ain't movin'. You know the rules. You don't like it – *you* take a hike."

"I have no intention of moving."

"Sylvester," I said, "Would *you* like to move to a different room."

"Hell, no. I been here four years." He poked his finger into the crumpled sheets on his bed, "This is my home."

"And how long have you been here?" I asked Jacob.

"Five years."

"So you've been roommates for quite some time. Do either of you think it's time for a change?"

Sylvester shook his head and Jacob said, "I guess not. I'm use to him. If I moved I'd just have to get use to someone else's slovenly ways." After taking a sip of tea he said, "The devil you know is better than the devil you don't know."

"What do you mean by that? Huh?" Sylvester hefted himself off the bed and lumbered over to his side of the black tape on the floor, being careful not to cross the line.

Jacob waved his hand at the posters thumb tacked to the walls on Sylvester's side of the room. Posters of hulking, muscle-bound wrestlers in menacing poses.

"Oh yeah? Look what I have to put up with." Sylvester jabbed his hand at the oils that hung on Jacob's side of the room. Scenes of meadows and seascapes.

"Think it over," I said. "I'll come back and we'll talk again."

When we were back in the hall I said, "Well? How did I do?"

"Your life's not going to get any easier," Ruby said.

By the time Apolonia called on her lunch hour I had done another psychosocial history on a patient who had been admitted later in the morning and was almost done with the care plans. "There are advantages to working here, Apolonia," I said, "Where else but in a nursing home would a woman my age be called a kid?"

"So, you like the job."

"I wouldn't go that far," I said. "I couldn't make a room change and I don't understand why not and, most of my morning was drone work. Have you ever done care plans?"

"We don't call them that here but I know what you mean."

I flexed my hand as we talked, trying to work out a cramp. "Judy told me I have to get something on every care plan before the state surveyors come in, and she says this afternoon I can start on the charts. This isn't why I became a social worker, Apolonia. How's your job going?"

"Okay, I guess," she sighed, "I talked that woman with the three obnoxious kids into packing up and going to a safe house. Again. I felt like I was making gains until my boss told me the Tattooed Wonder will find her and she'll go back."

"You sound discouraged." A wave of guilt swept over me as I held my breath waiting for her to say she was resigning.

Instead she said, "Apparently they give this case to every new social worker. I feel like a salmon swimming upstream. But the benefits are great. And it's kind of like starring in an afternoon soap opera. I guess. What's new with you besides paperwork?"

"An administrator." The new administrator, Mr. Montgomery, was a short, rotund, rosy-cheeked man with a barking laugh. "I haven't seen much of him but, he seems nice and we seem to hit it off," I said. "So far."

"Of course," Apolonia said. "You're both new kids on the block."

"Kids? He's got to be in his late fifties. Nappy dresser. Bow ties. Wears his hat at an angle."

"Watch out. My Uncle Al wore his hat like that."

"So?"

"So he had a heart attack and died in bed. With another woman. Aunt Sadie wanted to kill him."

Twenty-One

By the end of the first week Maxine had turned me over to Kathleen, the activities director. Kathleen was a short, plump woman with wide green eyes, masses of unruly blond curls, and belts cinched so tightly that her hips and bosom flared out like an hourglass. She had the startled look of someone who was about to gasp for air after holding her breath too long. "Document as though a friendly jury was looking over your shoulder," she told me, "and keep it short. One line. Sum up what happened. What you said. What they said. Put it in quotes. And, if there's a problem, make sure you document the solution or the state will get you."

In the short time I had been there, the state had become an ever-present boogieman. The vacuum cleaner was in constant use while agitated residents writhed in their chairs, clawing out hearing aids and hiding them in wads of tissue paper, which they later threw away. Half-eaten sandwiches and cold pizzas were removed from the refrigerators behind the nurses' stations where some of the medicine was stored, and the lawns and bushes were groomed and regroomed. Cigarette butts outside the front door, spills and discarded tissues on the floors, and short shorts on the nurses' aides were added to the list of mortal sins that Judy hung in the employee's bathrooms. In big red letters someone had scrawled at the top of the list: The State Is Coming – Are *YOU* Ready? Kathleen took this personally because the state always met with the residents' council and the residents' council was in disarray. Kathleen groaned and buried her nail-bitten fingers in her hair. "It's Paul," she said. "Now that he's feeling better he's taking over the council. He found out that one of the nurses is dating a guy who's a union organizer and he had the residents vote on whether or not we should be unionized. He made up the ballots and zeroxed them on the business office copier. He's even making up bumper stickers for people's wheelchairs and walker baskets."

By Friday night I knew the names of most of the day staff and the background histories on several of the residents - especially the residents who had been admitted to Churchill Lake when the nursing home first opened and psychosocial intakes were written as narratives instead of the generic checklists that replaced them.

When I read Rose Walsh's history I discovered that Peter Michael's sophisticated and aloof great-aunt looked on her great-nephew as the grandchild she never had. He chose the cartoon-emblazoned sweat suits she wore, and the enameled, primary-colored furniture in her corner of the room. The corkboard at the foot of her bed was covered with gifts from Peter Michael. Get well cards and photos of cloudless skies, or expanses of grass with blurry images of a camera shy cat disappearing from the frame of several pictures. There were snapshots and school pictures of Peter Michael and there were pictures he had drawn. "He's an artist," she said one afternoon pointing to one of the pictures. "That's my favorite. We crayon together when he comes in, but that one he did especially for me when he went fishing with his grandfather." The sketch was of a large figure in the back of a canoe and a smaller figure up front, who was paddling them away from the gaping jaws of an enormous duck. "The one doing the paddling is Peter Michael. He's rescuing me from the Loch Ness Monster."

"Oh, the Loch Ness Monster!"

"He brought those back from his vacation in Maine," she said, pointing to three smooth white stones resting on the window ledge beside her bed. "Do you know what they are?"

There was a pang of recognition so strong my heart ached.

"Lucky stones," I said. "My brother Brian used to give them to mother when we were children. She used to keep them on the windowsill by her bed."

"I'll bet she's still got them." After a while, when I didn't answer, she said, "He thinks they're going to make me well again. Do you believe in lucky stones?"

I shook my head.

"Neither do I."

I picked up one of the small, cool stones and turned it over in the palm of my hand. Brian had always collected his stones in the woods behind our house, the woods he was forbidden to play in unless I went with him.

"I'm not going to make it," she said softly. "My veins have collapsed and they want to put in a central line here." She lifted her hand to the area near her collarbone. "I'm not going to let them do it. I'm so tired I just want to let go, but I can't because I don't know how Peter Michael will cope."

"How can I help?" I asked, sitting down on the edge of her bed.

She took the stone from my hand and closed her fist around it. "Help him get through this. You're a social worker. You'll know what to do."

When I told Maxine about our conversation she said, "Be careful. When you're sittin' with dyin' patients you've always got to remember that hearing's the last thing to go. We had this guy who was terrified of dyin'. There was a nor'easter on the day he went sour. The snow was up ta here," she tapped her broad chest. "Some of the staff couldn't make it in 'cause the roads weren't plowed, so the nurses were workin' short. I sat with him. When I was sure we were alone," she looked up and down the empty hall, then leaned closer and lowered her voice, "I asked him if when he saw God that afternoon he'd ask 'im to

let me win Megabucks."
   "Did you win?"
   "Hell no. He rallied."

Twenty-Two

Maryanne had begun putting in more hours at the restaurant. When she wasn't working in the kitchen, she was waiting on tables or mixing drinks behind the bar. When I urged her to slow down she said it was all good experience and would pay off when she opened her own restaurant. After that, she began to avoid me.

On the rare occasions when our paths crossed, I noticed she looked paler than usual. Twice I heard her vomiting in the bathroom as I got ready for work.

Apolonia didn't help to ease my concerns when she said, "Vomiting in the morning. Hmmmm." We were sitting at a table in the day room waiting to discuss her father's care plan with the team. The therapists hadn't shown up yet and the nurses were busy finishing paperwork so they could transfer a resident to the hospital for x-rays after a fall. Marilyn, who had heard the call for the ambulance on her citizen's band radio, was already sitting by the front door applying a fresh coat of cherry red lipstick and tugging at her neckline.

Kathleen settled herself at the table and began updating the activities calendar. "Vomiting in the morning?'" she said. "Wow, sometimes that goes on for the whole nine months." She tossed her head and tried to tame the masses of wild curls by tucking her hair behind her ears, then patted Apolonia's hand, "But don't worry, honey. It's all worth it in the end when you see that beautiful little baby."

"Not *me,*" Apolonia said, pulling her hand away. "Gloria's daughter."

Kathleen got up and hugged me. "Congratulations."

I pushed her away. "My daughter's not pregnant." Apolonia and Kathleen exchanged a look. "She's not," I said.

"Okay," Kathleen said, "Okay, relax." She was just sitting down as Ruby pushed Apolonia's dad into the room. He winked at Kathleen and tried to touch her bottom as his wheelchair rolled by her chair.

"*Dad!*" Apolonia blushed.

"That's okay." Kathleen fluttered her fingers and laughed. "I'm used to it,"

"My father was *never* like that. He never drank. He never swore. And, he *certainly* never made passes at women he didn't know." She straightened in her chair, and the camaraderie she and Kathleen had just shared at Maryanne's expense evaporated, as she looked Kathleen over from head to toe, pausing at the flared hips and bosom, before giving me a meaningful look.

"It's not just me," Kathleen said. "He does the same thing to Mrs. Grinshaw, and she's 102 and refuses to wear her dentures or shave her chin." Apolonia's dad ducked his head and grinned.

"As his dementia progresses he loses his inhibitions," Ruby said. "We redirect him or keep him by the nurse's station where we can keep an eye on him. This isn't unusual."

"His *dementia*?"

From that point on the meeting went downhill fast. The staff had become Apolonia's enemy, and I was in their camp. The original plan had been for short-term rehab and a return home, but since the original stroke a series of smaller silent strokes had begun to rob his memory. After a CAT scan, a diagnosis of vascular dementia had been added. In the staff's opinion, a return home would be unsafe. "We'll keep assessing him," Ruby said.

"I live with my father," Apolonia said. "I can take care of him."

"Can you be there twenty-four hours a day, seven days a week?" Ruby asked. She turned to Apolonia's dad. "Mr. Farintino, if there was a fire in the house and you were home alone, what would you do?"

He grinned. "I'd ask Kathleen to help me."

Kathleen patted his hand. "But if I wasn't there, Mr. Farintino, and you were home all alone, what would you do?"

"Turn off the toaster."

Kathleen turned to Apolonia and shrugged.

"You're the discharge planner," Apolonia shouted at me. "Get him out of here. Can't you see what's happening to him? He's getting worse, not better. I want him home. I don't want him spending the rest of his days making passes at the Bingo Queen." She nodded in Kathleen's direction.

"He came here because he was beginning to fail," Ruby said. "Since he's been here he's had a series of silent strokes. His disease is progressing."

"I want him home," Apolonia said.

"I'll keep assessing him," I said.

Apolonia stood up so quickly her chair fell to the floor. "That's it," she said. "You've had your chance. I'm getting him out of here and I'm getting him someplace where they can do something for him and get him home. Don't you worry, Daddy." She hugged him fiercely and then stalked to the door, "I'll get you home."

After she left the room there was a moment of silence. Then Apolonia's father said, "Who *was* that?"

Twenty-Three

Later that night Apolonia called to apologize. "This job is getting to me," she said, "Everything's out of my control. At home. At work. That woman moved back with her husband. It's bad enough he shaves his head but he wears these scary black boots. He calls them 'shitkicker boots.' The kids are terrified of him."

"Can't you get the kids out of there?"

"Didn't you hear what I just said? That guy scares me, Gloria. As vague as Dad is, he'd at least be a male presence in the house. Now I'm alone."

"Maryanne's buying a house maybe you can move in there. Or move in with us if you're afraid."

"I'm not that afraid. Not yet. I'm not going to let some skinhead scare me out of my home."

"Then get a dog. A big one."

Twenty-Four

We made plans to go to the pound the next day after work, but the state survey team arrived and I had to stay until they left for the evening.

The beginning of the survey was announced on the overhead page when the three surveyors walked into the building before our morning meeting. All department heads were paged to the conference room. I was the first staff member to arrive, and sat at the long table next to a tall, thin, balding man wearing a pin-stripped suit and a pained expression. When I tried to look over his hunched shoulders at the papers he was shuffling through, he turned them over. The other two surveyors were grim-faced women. The older one, a fierce-looking blond, asked me, "Is this 'Churchill Nursing Home' or 'Churchill Nursing House?'"

I thought she was kidding. "Put down 'Home,'" I said. "It sounds cozier."

She filled out a few more lines of her form and put down the pen. "Where are the others?" she asked me.

The man snorted. "In an office somewhere, figuring out their strategy," he said.

As the day wore on I began to realize that, despite the initial iciness, my first survey was going well. The third woman surveyor told me she was impressed with my care plans. The man, who turned out to be a social worker, said they were all impressed that I had managed to connect with so many residents and staff in such a short time.

Everyone felt self-conscious and suddenly aware of how familiar routines might look to an outsider.

Sylvester and Jacob hid the black tape that divided their room under wrestling posters and oil paintings. The maintenance man removed the tape from the floor.

Maxine and Kathleen came into my room at lunchtime to escape the tension. "During a survey every nursin' home's like the Titanic," said Maxine. "If ya think ya might be on a sinkin' ship, ya bond fast and tight. You save my ass, I'll save yours."

"Right, Max," Kathleen said. "But didn't the people in the lifeboats use axes to chop off the hands of anyone in the water who tried to climb in?"

Maxine raised her eyebrows "Ya see any axes in here? I don't."

Lucy, an Italian lady who favored baggy gray sweaters and slipper socks, occasionally locked herself in the unit kitchen. She had been warned repeatedly not to use the microwave to brew herbal tea or make popcorn. Since she spoke no English and the staff spoke no Italian they grew adept at pantomiming steam, boiling water and burning flesh while shouting, "Vesuvius! Etna!" and waving their arms to indicate volcanic eruptions. Lucy shrugged off the warnings, but learned to make sure no one was watching when she slipped in to use the microwave.

On the first day of the survey I had just explained to the blond surveyor that Lucy understood English, although she didn't speak it, when Lucy shuffled out of the kitchen and over to where we were sitting. After a furtive glance down the hallway, she flashed opened her sweater to show us that the bulge beneath her sweater was a bag of freshly popped popcorn. "Shhh," she said. "Surveyors!" She passed the popcorn to us and acted as lookout while we each took a handful. Then she put the popcorn under her sweater and shuffled off her room to stash it in her closet. "I see what you mean," said the surveyor.

There were close calls. On the second day, the nurse who was dating a union organizer threw a calcified hotdog under the stove in the kitchen in an effort to get the home written up for a food safety violation. Peter Michael's calico cat managed to tease it out while the blond surveyor was examining the temperature of the freezers. Peter Michael saw the hotdog, snatched it up, put it in his backpack and was gone before the surveyor came out of the freezer.

Through it all, Mr. Montgomery, the new administrator who was nick-named Kewpie because of his striking resemblance to the doll of the same name, strolled through the nursing home, glad-handing everyone he met and managing to hide the fact that he, like me, hadn't had time to learn the layout of the building or to meet many of the employees. He put his hand firmly on the shoulder of each employee he encountered, made intense eye contact, and said, "How's it going?" Without waiting for a reply he would add, "You're doing great. Just great." This was a tremendous relief to the staff who didn't know him and thought he was one of the surveyors.

Maxine was gracious. Kathleen loosened up her belts. Marilyn toned down her makeup. And Apolonia's dad only made one pass at a surveyor – the male social worker.

On the third day, I went downstairs to tell the administrator that Marilyn had heard the surveyors say they planned to leave the building that afternoon. Mr. Montgomery was in his office, leaning against the wall. His eyes were closed. He was breathing in through his nose, out through pursed lips. His hand was splayed against his chest. "Are you okay?" I asked.

He opened his eyes, smiled, put his hand on my shoulder and said, "How's it going? You're doing great. Just great."

We all knew the survey had gone well, so by the time the written results were received, a party on the patio was planned, champagne was ordered, and the invitations were stamped and waiting to be mailed. And I was beginning to feel like a social worker.

Twenty-Five

After Tony and Kevin finished winterizing Mom's room and the beige rug had been installed, Maryanne painted the woodwork white. Then she and I papered the walls with white-on-white wallpaper and finished it off with a border of gulls and lighthouses. Apolonia and I became experts at negotiating yard sales. Tony stripped and varnished a rocker we found and put new hardware on the dresser and sleigh bed we brought home in Kevin's pickup, and we all helped move the piano from the living room to the bedroom. The gas log fireplace was installed on the afternoon when the first of Mom's boxes arrived from Florida.

Apolonia came over that night to help me unpack. As soon as Maryanne and Kevin had gone off to pick up the door for the bedroom she said, "She's pregnant."

"You're wrong. I'm her mother. I'd be the first to know."

"The mother's the last to know. You worked with teenaged mothers. You know the drill."

"She's not a teenager."

"Okay. But she's pregnant. I'll bet you a pepperoni pizza she is."

"You're probably right, I've been trying to broach the subject with her for a week. When I finally asked her outright if she was pregnant, she put her hand on her chest and said, *"Mom!"*

"When was that?" Apolonia asked.

"Last night."

"Good. You softened her up. I'll go in for the kill. When they get back I'll make up some excuse to get her alone and find out. I'll let you know."

After Kevin and Maryanne got home, Apolonia said she was

going out to pick up extra hangers and asked Maryanne to come along. The door was up, the boxes were unpacked, and I was arranging Mom's lucky stones on the windowsill beside the sleigh bed when Apolonia came back in. Kevin looked up from his toolbox, "Where's Maryanne?" he asked.

"Up in her room," Apolonia said, "She wants to talk to you."

Kevin snapped the latches on his toolbox and said softly, "Is she all right?"

"She's fine. She just wants to talk to you. Alone. That's all."

A feeling of numbness started in my heart and began to spread though my body. "Maybe I should go up," I said.

"Not now, Gloria." Apolonia took me by the arm and led me out to her car.

"What?" I said, once we were outside the house.

"I'm buying you a drink and *then* we'll talk."

"That bad, huh?" The compassion in Apolonia's eyes confirmed what I already knew. "I like Kevin," I said. "But I wanted Maryanne to go to college before she got married and settled down. Or," I glanced over at Apolonia, "had a baby."

The Mexican restaurant was crowded, so we waited in the bar for a table to open on the patio. The waitress pushed her way through the noisy crowd and slapped a small wooden square down in front of us. "Don't lose this," she shouted. "When your table's ready those little red knobs light up, and that's how I can find you in this bar. She took a small notepad from her pocket and looked around the pulsating room. "God, it's noisy in here tonight."

"Two martinis," Apolonia shouted.

"What?" the waitress shouted back, leaning over so her ear was an inch from Apolonia's mouth.

"Two martinis."

"Gotcha." She scribbled on her notepad and turned to walk

away, but Apolonia hooked her thumb in the waitress' pocket and shouted, "That's for *her*. I'll have rum and coke."

The waitress scribbled on her notepad again and disappeared into the crowd. I leaned across the table and shouted, "Is she?"

Apolonia shook her head, "Yup," she shouted back, "Yup. You're going to be a grandmother." She looked at me and smiled, then looked past me to the end of the bar. The terror in her eyes made me turn. A tall muscular man standing at the end of the bar slid a dirty baseball cap over his shaved head and nodded to Apolonia. Without losing eye contact with her, he kicked the door behind him open and then turned. Suddenly the wooden square wobbled across the bar as the small red lights blinked on and off in time to a loud, tinny syncopated tune. Startled, we both reached out to keep it from falling to the floor. When we looked up, a laughing crowd was jostling its way through the door.

"Where is he?" I said.

"I don't know, but that was him," Apolonia whispered, craning her neck and looking around the crowded bar. "Oh, my God. That was him."

Twenty-Six

In September after school opened, James' wife called and said she was no longer able to be home to "keep an eye on your mother."

"She's James' mother, too," I said.

"Sure she is, but you know how it goes. I'm sure you run into it a lot at that nursing home where you work, Gloria. A parent could have eight healthy sons and one daughter who's on oxygen and confined to a wheelchair, but who do you think would get stuck taking care of mom?"

"Are you saying you feel stuck?"

"No. You're not hearing me. That's not what I said."

"Then what *did* you say?"

"I said I feel trapped. James switched to nights so that he could watch her during the day, and now he's doing double shifts. I hardly ever see him. It's not helping our relationship. When I get home my life revolves around correcting papers and watching either the food channel or some nun lecture on art. And she's addicted to *I Love Lucy* reruns. I can't take it any more, Gloria. It's like James and I are ships that pass in the night. I'm going nuts."

It might have been September in Florida, but an icy frost whooshed through the phone lines and up the Eastern seaboard. James and his wife may have been looking forward to having the house to themselves again, but at our home it was as though we were preparing for the arrival of a potentate.

On Saturday I cleaned the house from attic to basement until the windows sparkled and the speckled gray interior of the oven looked like new. I even color-coordinated the plastic hangers in mom's closet and pressed all the curtains, upstairs and down.

That night I was overtired and had a hard time falling asleep.

When I did finally doze off around two in the morning, I slipped into a nightmare and woke up from a dream so real that I felt my heart pounding in my chest and could hardly breathe. I had dreamed that a mass murderer was on the loose while I calmly ironed sheets in the upstairs bedroom. When I looked out the window towards the far end of the street I noticed police, paired in twos, searching methodically through houses and yards. Some wore suits and badges flashed on their belts; others were in full uniform. They were several houses away and their approach was agonizingly slow. Most of the police were faceless but some I recognized. Ray was up and walking beside Kevin while Apolonia checked the trashcans and bushes carefully. James' wife in her S.W.A.T. uniform and Maxine, also in full uniform and wearing a black helmet, were urging an elderly woman to go back inside her house.

In my dream I suddenly remembered that Maryanne was alone in the living room. I rushed to the top of the stairs to warn her there was a mass murderer in the neighborhood, but when I leaned over the banister I saw that Maryanne, dressed in a bridal gown, was laughing with a tall, bald man who had a tattoo on the nape of his neck. I rushed back to the bedroom trying to decide whether I should shut and lock the door or call out to warn her. As I reached for the deadbolt on the door, I woke up. I concentrated on my breathing and finally calmed the heavy pounding in my chest but stayed awake till the rising sun glimmered through the spotless windows.

The night before Mom's arrival Maryanne told me she was going to press Mom's sheets before she made the bed. "Don't look so shook up, Mom," she said, "I'm not going to make a habit of this. I just thought it would help Nana get off to a good start."

"It's not that," I said.

"Then what is it? You look terrible. Are you feeling all right?"

She listened as I told her about my dream, then snapped a sheet over the ironing board and plugged in the iron. "Mom," she said, with infinite patience, "Get a grip. You don't have to worry about everything. Let it go. I'm fine. Apolonia's fine. And mom will be fine once she gets here tomorrow. You're taking this social work thing too seriously." She touched the tip of her finger to her tongue and then touched the iron quickly. "And what's the deal about me in a wedding dress?"

"Well?"

"Well what?"

The phone rang and I took the iron from her when she went into the other room to answer it. While I smoothed the iron over the sheet I tried to listen to her side of the conversation. She was arguing with Kevin. Maryanne had begun giving in to her internal hormonal roller coaster, and Kevin seemed to be having a hard time hanging on during the precipitous drops in her mood. I began to worry because there were no discussions about a wedding and no plans for a nursery. Each time we talked I felt like Maryanne was a wild bird that I was trying to lure into the palm of my hand.

When she came back into the kitchen, I could see that she had been crying.

"What is it?" I asked.

"Nothing."

"Are you sure?"

"Mom, I'm all right. Back off."

She went up to her room and didn't come back downstairs until I began making the bed in Mom's room. "I'm sorry," she said, taking one side of the sheet and helping me snap it over the mattress. "I don't know what's wrong with me anymore."

"You've got a lot on your mind." She nodded. "How's the bed and breakfast coming along?"

"It's coming along," she said.

"Any plans for a nursery?" I hadn't realized she had invited Kevin over to the house until I saw him standing in the doorway behind her, covered in sawdust, his work boots unlaced and his dirty T-shirt soaked in sweat. Kevin grinned and gave me two thumbs up.

"*Mom!*" she said, "We just finished *this* room, and I'm getting the damn *restaurant* ready over at the *bed and breakfast*. I can only take so *much*. I'm *human,* you know." She began to sob, hurling throw pillows onto the bed as though she were trying to kill them.

"Honey?" Kevin said softly.

Maryanne was holding the last of the throw pillows. For a moment, I thought she was going to throw it at Kevin. Instead, she laid it gently on the bed and, still sobbing, walked into his open arms.

"Kevin," I said, "you should have been the social worker, not me."

Twenty-Seven

I was having more success at work than I was at home. Ray had allowed himself to be taken to a church service one Monday morning, which I considered a personal victory. That afternoon I sat down beside his bed to visit while he ate his lunch.

"I'm glad you're going to church, Ray," I said. He looked at me for a long time then spooned a helping of soup into his mouth. Uncomfortable with long pauses during conversations, I said, "I thought you were a Catholic."

"Yup," he finally said.

"That was a Protestant service." I shifted my weight from one hip to the other and crossed my legs. Waiting. "I mean that's okay and everything. I just wanted to make sure…."

"I know." He held his spoon halfway to his mouth, making intense eye contact while we waited. Finally he said, "Ya find the watch yet?"

"Not yet. But I'm still looking."

"Good." He went back to his soup. We both knew the visit had been successful but, it was over.

It wasn't until the next Monday morning, when I saw Mr. Montgomery standing in front of the large window that formed one wall of the activities room, that I found out the real reason for Ray's spiritual reawakening.

"What does she do with that veil? And why is she barefoot?" Mr. Montgomery asked.

"What veil?" I asked. Usually my Monday mornings were spent on the units getting an update from the nurses and visiting with bed-bound residents. I stood beside him and together we looked through the window.

A plump woman wearing a floral dress and a small purple

hat peered over the top of her glasses at sheet music while playing the organ. Occasionally she fumbled for a missed chord, smiling to herself when she retrieved it. In the middle of the floor, surrounded by a circle of residents, a middle-aged, athletic-looking woman with a bright smile, long, slim arms and gray hair that reached to her hips swayed to the hymn *How Great Thou Art*. She lifted an iridescent veil high above her head, then slowly lowered both arms to her sides and rolled her head in dreamy circles, first to one side and then to the other.

Mr. Montgomery clasped his hands behind his back and leaned forward, his breath steaming the window as the woman rolled her feet from toe to heel and side to side in time to the music.

"Relax Mr. Montgomery, she's not going to do anything with that veil." He straightened up and looked over at me. "It looks like yoga to me," I said.

"Ahhh," Mr. Montgomery's laughter was short and crisp, "You're right. Good for you. My trophy wife was a yoga teacher."

"Your trophy wife?"

"She was fun." He closed his eyes, threw his arms up and swiveled his head and hips, then clasped his hands behind his back again and gazed through the window with a smile. "But she was too much for me. I got lucky though. My first wife took me back, God bless her."

Twenty-Eight

Although they weren't in the job description, I began to find myself making a lot of side trips to do errands for residents. Besides searching for Ray's watch, I bought clothing for Rowena, who had managed to alienate her only relative, a daughter who had moved to the opposite coast, bought an answering machine and then refused to answer it. When I contacted the friend listed on the face sheet of Rowena's chart, I found out the friend had been paid by the daughter to help with housework and shopping before the elderly woman had been admitted to Churchill Lake.

"What are ya complain' about?" Maxine said, "We had a male social worker here once. Howie. Tough little Portuguese guy with a beard and moustache. He looked like an escapee from a gangster movie. Talked tough. Looked tough. Was tough. Used to come to work on his Harley Davidson. But ya didn't hear *him* whinin' when *he* had ta go shoppin'. He bought ladies' underwear, in all different sizes. Pocket books. Dresses. Howie even used to pick up wigs once in a while. The clerks at WalMarts had a bet goin' that he was a real ugly transvestite with no class - no sense of size or style."

"Was he one of the ones the administrator harassed?"

"Yeah. He called him into his office and gave him hell for not doing enough for the residents. After an hour, Howie had enough. He popped 'im one. Gave up social work and went back to teachin' woodworkin' in a prison. Said it was easier." She lowered her head and pointed a finger at me. "But don't get any funny ideas. We all need ya here, Gloria. Ya even managed to calm down Jacob that night Sylvester's army buddies came in to watch the football game and drink beer."

"Yes. But the next day when Jacob's friends came in to play bridge, Sylvester called them pansies."

"Hey," Maxine said, "Ya win some - ya lose some."

Twenty-Nine

I realized how much I was needed when I came into work one morning and found Maxine and Judy waiting in my office. Judy was sitting on the couch leafing through a dog-eared People magazine. Maxine was sitting behind my desk chewing gum, but when I came in to the room she dropped her feet to the floor, spit her gum into the wastebasket, and moved to the couch.

"What's up?" I asked.

Judy closed the magazine with a sigh. "You've got to do something about the gift shop."

"That's Kathleen's problem. She's the activities director. She's in charge of the gift shop."

"Well, she's part of the problem. Have you noticed that lately Paul's been running the shop?"

"So?"

"So, it took her years –"

"Eight years, to be exact," Maxine interrupted, patting her pockets for the reassurance that she hadn't forgotten her cigarettes.

"– to get her volunteers together. And they were loyal. Weren't they, Max?" Max nodded. "Until Paul fired them."

"All of 'em," Max said. She tucked an unlit cigarette into the corner of her mouth and talked around it. "Ya see, this is the problem." She leaned forward and rested her elbows on her knees. "Not only did he fire all the volunteers, but he's snaggin' anybody who walks by the gift shop, and once they're in there he doesn't let 'em out until they buy something."

"Usually something they don't need, don't want, or can't afford," Judy said, playing with the row of earrings on her ear. "He likes you, Gloria. Talk to him. Kathleen doesn't get anywhere with him because she just becomes hysterical, and then he tries to calm her down, and then she becomes enraged, and it just goes on and on."

"Maybe people should just ignore him and walk a little faster," I said.

Maxine pulled the cigarette from the corner of her mouth and leaned back, "'Walk a little faster'?" she said. "Most of the people in this place couldn't walk a little faster if their ass was on fire." Mr. Montgomery chose that moment to walk into my office, overhearing the last part of our conversation.

"Maxine, you deal with the public," he began.

"And the place is full, right?" Maxine looked a little worried.

"I'm not denying that. You're very good at what you do," Mr. Montgomery said. "But what I was *going* to say was, charm us with your colorful language and spare the public."

"Gotcha," Maxine said. Without thinking she put her cigarette back in her mouth and lit it. When Mr. Montgomery's eyes widened, she pulled a crushed pack of Camels from her pocket, shook one up, and offered it to him. Judy rolled her eyes when he took it, lit up, and blew a perfect circle of blue smoke above her head.

Thirty

Mom moved back on Sunday. By Monday, she and Ida were on the phone and the wedding machine had begun to roll. Ida suspected what Mom knew, and with Mom's encouragement Maryanne and Kevin met with Ida and told her they were expecting. "I've learned to expect the unexpected," Ida said. "Two weeks after your mother and father got married, your Aunt Vivian and Uncle Ralph ran off to Reno and got married in some chapel with a neon sign and a justice of the peace who looked like Little Richard. Nothing surprises me anymore. The only problem I have is, what comes first? The baby shower or the wedding?"

Maryanne gave her notice at the restaurant and began spending her days and evenings at the bed and breakfast. Some nights she and Kevin slept there. Their plan was to open the restaurant for a trial run on the Thanksgiving weekend but wait until the following spring to rent the rooms and open the restaurant full time.

Tony and Kevin had rescued a scarred red piano from a local barroom they were renovating, replaced the missing ivory on several of the keys, and had it tuned.

When Mom heard them discussing plans to hire someone to play show tunes in the dining room she said, "Can I audition?"

"Nana, we'll need a jazz pianist."

"I can do that," she said. "Why spend money for something when I'd do it for free? Besides, it'll be good therapy for my wrist." The piano and Mom turned out to be a perfect match. "Of course," Mom said, patting the piano tenderly. "We were two lost souls saved from the brink of extinction."

The sound of hammering, sawing and old show tunes or Joplin rags began to catch the attention of people passing by who often stopped to see what was happening in the big white house with the dark green shutters and red window boxes. Mom began giving impromptu tours, asking everyone who had taken the tour to leave a business care in a straw basket near the front door.

"What's that all about?" I asked Mom, as we sat down at the kitchen counter to sample one of Maryanne's meals.

"I've been telling everyone that we're raffling off a free night's stay once *Just for Tonight* opens this spring.

"*Just for Tonight?*" Maryanne asked, pulling over a stool and joining us at the counter.

"Of course," Mom said. "It's a white house. It has green shutters and red window boxes. What else would you call it? It'll be like Christmas all year round."

"Christmas all year round," Maryanne said, chewing slowly as she thought it over. "That might work."

"Of course it'll work," Mom said. "Gloria, remember when you were little and I read that poem to you before you went to bed on Christmas Eve? 'Backward, turn backward, oh time in thy flight. Make me a child again, just for tonight.'"

Maryanne reached across the table and took my hand, "And Mom read it to me every Christmas Eve. I loved it. What do you think, Mom?" she said.

"That would make a wonderful cross-stitch sampler to put near the front door."

"We could soak it in tea and distress a frame so that it looked like something we had found hidden away in the attic," Maryanne said.

Mom winked and said, "I have great ideas, don't I?" She took a bite from her meal. "What is this?"

"Cavatappi with roast chicken and vegetables," Maryanne said. "You like it?"

"Like it? I love it. It's a lot better than that steak au poivre with peppercorns falling off all over the place."

"By the time we get *Just for Tonight* up and running the peppercorns will stay on," Maryanne said.

Mom looked across the table and smiled. "Aren't you glad I'm here?"

Thirty-One

Maryanne was especially glad that Mom was living with us.

Kevin worked days for Tony. In the evenings and on weekends the two of them, along with several of Tony's crew, hung missing shutters and replaced broken windows and doors at the bed and breakfast. Maryanne stayed home while the floors were sanded and the woodwork painted. Since I often worked late as I struggled to learn my job, her relationship with Mom deepened as the two of them hemmed curtains or pored over cookbooks.

"Nana came up with another great idea," Maryanne said one evening as we worked on a patchwork quilt for the baby's crib. "Once we get the place open, she says, we should pack picnic hampers for guests who want to take a lunch to the beach or a breakfast to Brewster Park. We're going to do a test run this weekend. Want to come along?"

"Sure," I said.

Maryanne packed a large wicker hamper with coffee, juice, fresh strawberries and oversized blueberry muffins on Sunday morning. By the time we had walked over to Brewster Park, Kevin had laid out the blanket and was setting up folding chairs. Ida was still at Mass, and Tony had driven over to the church to pick her up.

"What a beautiful place," Mom said. "Look at how that tree branch is bent. It looks like it's bowing down to the river. And that lovely little bridge." A wedding party posed for a photographer on a narrow wooden bridge that arched over a fast-moving, spring-fed stream. Gulls circled overhead and the flower girls, tripping over their dresses and tumbling into the bushes, played tag nearby.

The groom saw Kevin and stepped around the photographer, crossing the grass with his arms outstretched. "You son of a gun!" he called out, startling a duck and her brood, who waddled out of his way and slipped into the water. Kevin slapped him on the back, and they walked towards the edge of the stream with their arms over each other's shoulders. The groom looked back at us several times, each time nodding approvingly at Maryanne, who was busy laying out the breakfast linen and plates. Mom waved. The groom waved back and was about to come over when the bride called to him from the bridge. He shrugged, hugged Kevin, and turned away.

"Who was that, Kevin?" Mom asked, when he came back and stretched out on the blanket.

"A guy I went to grade school with. I haven't seen him in years."

"Do you believe in signs?" Mom said.

Kevin, knowing this could be a trick question, glanced at Maryanne. Her careful posture said it all: Watch out. "Maybe," he said. Maryanne shot him a murderous glance. "Or, then again, maybe not."

Mom frowned. "I do," she said. "Why do you think we saw a wedding today? And why do you think, of all the people in the world, the groom should be someone you know? Think about it."

Ida and Tony arrived as the wedding couple and flower girls were being helped into a white, horse-drawn carriage. As they drove away, Ida and Mom linked arms and walked over to the guests, who had broken into small groups to stroll along the narrow pathways or head for their cars. Mom and Ida stopped on either side of a woman in a lilac chiffon dress with an orchid corsage pinned at the shoulder. After a brief conversation she nodded and began scribbling notes on scraps of paper dug from the bottom of Mom's purse using the pen Ida had dug from her pocketbook.

"What do you think they're up to, Mom?" Maryanne said.

"Well, since they've been talking to somebody who's obviously the mother of the bride, my guess is that they're coming back with names and addresses of bridal shops and florists."

"Probably a caterer, too," Tony said.

"Shhh," I said, "here they are."

"Dad," Maryanne said, "I'm in the restaurant business. I *know* who I want to cater my wedding."

Ida hugged Maryanne and held out her arms to Kevin. "See, Ida?" Mom said. "They're thinking about a caterer. That's why I came back. They needed me to plan the wedding."

"Well, you can't do it alone," Ida said. "Look at all the work it took to get *our* kids married off."

"Grandma," Maryanne put her arm around Ida's waist, "we don't have a lot of money to spend on a wedding. We're fixing up the bed and breakfast, there's a baby on the way, all that's expensive. A wedding's just another day in your life. One day."

"No," mom said, "It's not just another day and it's not just one day. A wedding is the *first* day of forever. It's a commitment."

"And how much could it cost? Really?" Ida spread out her arms and turned around, "Look at this. And it's all free. We'll get Vinny –"

"Ma, Vinny's not a priest anymore," Tony said.

"Once a priest, always a priest. Besides, his twins would make wonderful flower girls. Five years old. They were perfect angels at you cousin Carmela's wedding. Maryanne, you can borrow Carmela's gown and veil. Look at how much money you've already saved."

"Oh, Ída," Mom said, "I'm so glad I'm back. It was so boring down in Florida. All I did was sit around and watch *I Love Lucy* reruns."

"When you weren't feeding alligators," Tony muttered under his breath.

Maryanne took Ida's hands in both of hers and said, "Grandma, the dress won't fit. Look at me. I'm pregnant."

"Perfect. So was Carmela."

Thirty-Two

We moved the sewing machine over to the bed and breakfast. The kitchen was complete and the restrooms nearly finished. Maryanne had bought plain white dishes at the Christmas Tree Shop, and while she stacked them in the cupboards I hung pots and pans from hooks on a rectangular iron rack suspended from the ceiling. When Mom and Ida weren't making curtains for the rooms upstairs they were arranging silk hydrangea blossoms in Mason jars and adding beaded ribbons. "So the rooms will look nice for the out-of-town relatives when they come for the wedding," Ida said. Because of the wedding, there had been pressure to finish some of the upstairs rooms before the spring.

A small room off the master bedroom was chosen for the nursery and filled with books and antique toys. "Do you think a kid would really enjoy playing with this stuff?" Apolonia said, holding up a small green paint chipped John Deere tractor. "This doesn't look healthy. Lead paint maybe. Let's get a few Barbies and Kens, just in case."

A finished carpenter who worked for Tony carved '*Just for Tonight*' into an oak panel designed to look like a cranberry-colored sleigh with miniature boxes and dolls piled high and spilling over the back.

On my lunch hours and on Saturdays Maxine and I began to search through yard sales and antique shops for Christmas music boxes and old-fashioned ornaments. When I told Maxine that Maryanne thought it might be a nice touch to have small artificial trees in each room, Maxine tacked up a notice on the bulletin board in the employee's lunchroom. For two weeks I drove home each night with the trunk of my car crammed with artificial and ceramic Christmas trees. Finally, Maxine posted another notice and the tree infestation stopped.

Kevin and Maryanne were looking for ornaments in one of the small shops downtown when they found their wedding rings instead. When Tony and I found out they had put them aside on lay-away, we decided to buy the rings as an early wedding gift. Apolonia came with me the day I went to pick them up.

Kevin's ring was a simple, wide gold band, but Maryanne had chosen a circlet of carved leaves and flowers. "Gorgeous," Apolonia said. Noticing an opal ring in the display case, she asked to see that one too, slipped it on her finger and held out her hand to admire the fire in the stone. "What do you think?" she said. "This or the ruby?" She pointed to another ring in the display case. "Can we see that one too?" Apolonia slipped the ring onto my finger, and I held out my hand next to hers.

The muffled ringing of a phone in an office at the end of the store caused the woman to look up. She nodded and whispered in a voice as smooth as chocolate, "Excuse me." Stepping from behind the counter, she raised a thin eyebrow at the owner of the shop, a tall, thin, elderly man. He smoothed his moustache and eased behind the counter to take her place, pretending to rearrange a display case while watching us from the corner of his eye.

Apolonia put her head close to mine and whispered, "We're making him nervous. We must look like a couple of jewel thieves." Then, in a louder voice she said, "You forgot your ski mask, Jackie? Well, then maybe we should just give the rings back." His smile tightened and he watched closely while we took off the rings and returned them to him.

"We're going to take the wedding rings," I said. "They're for my daughter and her fiancé."

While I wrote out the check he smiled at Apolonia. "Where are you getting married? In Vermont?" he asked.

Thirty-Three

Tony and I picked up tickets for the paddleboat sunset cruise and invited Kevin and Maryanne to join us. After a long hollow blast of its whistle followed by three short toots, the boat began to slowly pull away from the dock. Tony had already taken our waiter aside, given him the ring box, and asked him to bring it to the table with dessert. The pale blue sky was streaked with purple and the full white clouds were edged with gold from the setting sun by the time we finished the main course and the cherries jubilee arrived. Four small crystal bowls were arranged around a napkin folded into the shape of a swan. Nestled on the swan's back was the ring box.

"Oh, God," Maryanne said when she opened the box. "Oh, God." She hugged Kevin first, then Tony, then me. Then she hugged the waiter and said, "Do you want a job?"

"Sure," he said, "Where?"

"*Just for Tonight*," she said.

He held up his hands, shook his head and backed away. "I was thinking of something a little more permanent," he said.

Thirty-Four

When we got home the light on the answering machine was flashing. As I kicked off my shoes and took off my earrings I listened to Apolonia apologize. "I just got in from work and I dropped the groceries and couldn't get to the phone on time. I thought for sure you were still there. Oh, well. Try me again. I'll run faster next time. Sorry for babbling." The answering machine clicked off, and I erased the message.

Tony loosened his tie and unbuttoned his shirt. "With all that was going on tonight, when did you have time to call Apolonia?" he asked.

"I didn't. She's probably just laying a guilt trip on me because I was supposed to call her tonight to find out how she made out this afternoon." I padded into the kitchen and took a tub of ice cream out of the refrigerator. I handed one spoon to Tony and took one for myself, "Remember that family that's giving her so much grief?" Tony nodded, digging out a spoonful of ice cream. "She had to take the kids out of the house today. Had to take cops with her."

"Still sorry you didn't get that job?"

"I still think I should have gotten that job, Tony. That's not going to change. My job's okay, I suppose. I'm getting used to it. But I still want to work with kids," I spooned a dollop of ice cream into his mouth, "And right now I'm not exactly knee deep in kids, am I?"

"Hang on. We've got one on order, babe."

Thirty-Five

Apolonia seemed more relaxed the next time she came to visit her father at Churchill Lakes. She and her dad were eating pizza in his room and they invited me to join them. "Look at that," her dad said, pointing out the window. "There are cops all over the parking lot."

I crossed to the window and looked out. "What are the cops doing here?"

"You know that lady that goes around in an electric wheel chair and has a CB radio?" Apolonia said, "The one with tons of makeup and big boobs?"

"Big boobs?" her father said, putting aside his pizza.

"Marilyn," I said.

"Monroe?" her father said, "Is she here, too?"

"No, Dad." Apolonia took the slice of pizza from his hand and put in back in the cardboard box. "She saw someone in the bushes and called the police. I was scared to death until I found out it was only Ruby's husband."

"Jack Ruby?" her father said.

"No Dad. He's dead too."

"Marilyn Monroe's dead?"

Apolonia nodded and handed her father a Dixie cup of ginger ale.

"What a shame," he said, taking a sip and shaking his head.

"Her husband was gone by the time the police got here. I don't know why they're still poking around. There are still three police cars out there."

She came over and stood by my side as Maxine brought a family around the corner on a tour of the grounds.

"This ought to be good," Apolonia said.

The middle-aged man and the woman beside him froze

when they came face-to-face with the police. Maxine paused, stroked her chin for a moment, and then smiled sweetly. After making introductions all around, she strolled over to the nearest police car and opened the door. With a gracious sweep of her arm, she sent the officer in charge on his way. Car doors slammed and the procession of police cars drove off the grounds and out of sight. Maxine turned toward the window and winked.

Thirty-Six

Maryanne and I found a gallery uptown willing to let her display some of the work by local artists, each with a price tag tucked into a corner of a frame or on the base of a sculpture. "But that's not the best thing we found today," Maryanne said, while we unwrapped the paintings when we got home. "Look at this." Maryanne swirled a sleeveless ivory dress out of a crumpled brown shopping bag, shook it out, and held it toward Ida and Mom, who were tatting lace onto the edges of napkins.

Ida looked up. "What is it?" she asked.

Maryanne smoothed the wrinkled material against her body. "My wedding dress! Don't you love it?" The dress had a scoop neck, which was embroidered with green and black flowers.

"If you weren't pregnant," Ida said, "I'd say you had PMS. Dangerous PMS." She went back to her tatting. "Of course you're going to wear Carmela's dress."

"I want my own dress."

"Where did you find that one?" Ida asked, looking up from her work again.

"In *Yesterday's Fancies*."

"Isn't that the Salvation Army Store downtown? Why would you wear a stranger's dress when you could wear Carmela's dress?"

"It's that consignment shop next door to the art gallery. They're in the same building."

"It belonged to somebody who's not even a distant cousin. Not even a friend. A total stranger. When I was a young girl in school," Ida said, as her crochet hook tore back and forth, "the nuns told us about a young woman who wore someone else's wedding gown. A woman she didn't know, never met. She bought the dress in Filene's Basement."

Maryanne frowned. "How long ago was this, Grandma?"

Ida ignored her. "On the night of the wedding," she said, stopping her work and looking up to meet Maryanne's eyes, "she died." After Ida felt there had been enough time for that information to sink in she poked her glasses up further on the bridge of her glasses and looked down, and the crochet hook began to fly again. "Her family found out later that the dress had belonged to a young woman who died, and her family dressed her in the gown when she was laid out in her coffin. Formaldehyde poisoning." Maryanne sighed. "From my mouth to God's ear," Ida said. "A true story."

"Look, Grandma." Maryanne pulled up a chair and sat between Ida and Mom. "Look at the embroidery." She cupped the neckline of the dress in her hands and held it out for them to see. "Someone loved this dress. They did all that work by hand. Think of the love that went into that. And it's the same design as my ring, Nana. You both believe in signs. That's a sign."

"Weren't you with her?" Mom asked.

I shrugged and said, "It *is* the same design as the ring, which is really amazing. And retro's in this year."

"But Carmela's gown is perfect. It has hundreds of little seed pearls and the covered buttons up the back and a beautiful long train." Ida said.

"That train's so long it needs a caboose." Maryanne stamped from the room and slammed the front door on her way out so hard that windows banged shut with syncopated thuds throughout the house. Upstairs. Downstairs. In the hall.

"What a mouth on that one," Ida said. After a moment she added, "So she'll button up the train into a nice little bustle in the back."

By the time Maryanne let herself in quietly, after a stomp around the block, Mom had pressed the dress. As a peace offering, Ida volunteered to take up the hem. The windows were open again, propped up with wooden hangers.

Mom played the piano while Maryanne stood on a workbench in the middle of the restaurant rotating slowly. Ida clenched her lips around several straight pins, drawing them out one by one as she turned up the hem of the dress. Outside the open window, couples danced to the music.

Kevin had talked the waiter from the paddleboat into coming back to the bed and breakfast to get a feel for the restaurant. As they approached the crowd gathered near the window the waiter took the hand of a woman with a baby in a backpack and they began to dance as Mom launched into Joplin's *Original Rags*. Kevin strode up the front steps, motioning to the waiter to follow. "God! I feel like Gene Kelly," the waiter said, dancing up the steps behind him.

Mom had insisted that the gas log fireplace should be moved from her room to the bed and breakfast living room. Now it added to the atmosphere. The iron teakettle on top of the stove brewed cinnamon sticks in apple cider while Maryanne slowly turned in time to the music.

"Why do you want to show so much leg?" Ida asked Maryanne.

"If you've got it flaunt it, honey," the waiter said.

"Who's that?" Ida asked.

"Frank," the waiter said, crossing to Ida and shaking her hand. "What a great dress," he said to Maryanne. "It's so retro. That's in now."

"Another country heard from," Ida mumbled around the straight pins.

"It's not too much leg, Grandma," Maryanne said. "You're just bringing it up three inches above my ankle."

"That's an awkward length, Maryanne. How's that going to

look with heels? Even with flats it won't look right."

"I'm not wearing shoes, Grandma. I'm going barefoot."

"Barefoot! It's September! Do you want the baby to catch pneumonia? Kevin, talk to her."

"I'm going barefoot, too," he said.

The waiter looked puzzled, but before he could say anything more to Ida I offered to show him the rest of the house. His easy camaraderie was a bit dangerous, I thought, and it was better to redirect him so he couldn't say something that would set Maryanne off again.

The end of the tour sold Frank. We headed back to the restaurant to join the others, and Frank told us that he and a friend would help cater the wedding and he and his partner, Steve, would serve the guests.

"Don't I know you from somewhere?" Maryanne asked, "Didn't we work together briefly at *Lagastino's*?"

Frank snapped his fingers, "That's right. You worked in the bar when I was a waiter there. I thought I recognized you that night on the boat."

"And we both worked at the Chowder Fest last summer."

"Right again," Frank said. "Your restaurant won."

"That was my chowder recipe."

"Where's the reception going to be?"

"On Long Beach," Kevin said.

"I love it. When?"

"Next Sunday," Maryanne said, "It's kind of impromptu. That runs in our family."

"Whoa!"

"What? You can't manage it?"

"How many?"

Someone outside the window called in a request for *The Entertainer Rag.* As Mom swung into that song she called back over her shoulder, "Fifty, including the bride and groom."

"Can you do it on such short notice?" I asked.

"Consider it done," he said. "Oh, and by the way, it's a dining room, not a restaurant. There are thousands of restaurants in this town, but you guys are different. That's class."

Ida bit off the thread and held the dress out at arm's length. The corners of her mouth turned down with respect as she saw the simple elegance of the wedding gown for the first time. "*That's* class," she said softly.

Thirty-Seven

The next day when I went into work Ruby took me aside and said, "Rose is giving up. I think today's the day. We called her brother and he's in there now with Peter Michael, poor kid."

Rose had begun to withdraw from life soon after our conversation about Peter Michael, first by refusing medication and food and finally by refusing liquids. Eventually, she slept through visits. Even Peter Michael couldn't rouse her.

When I went into the room the calico cat was curled tightly against Rose's leg, its gentle purr lost in the hum of an oxygen tank. Her brother sat beside the bed and Peter Michael leaned against him, staring at Rose.

Knowing what a comfort it would be for Rose to hear the child's voice again, I said, "She can hear you."

Peter Michael shook his head and burrowed further against his grandfather, never taking his eyes from Rose.

"You want to hold her hand?" I asked. He shook his head. I reached over and began to pat her arm gently, slowly, until I noticed he was looking at my hand. "If you want to put your hand on top of mine, you can," I said.

Slowly he reached out and rested his hand lightly on top of mine. Together we patted Rose's arm until his fingers slipped off the edge of my hand. His fingertips dragged gently along the coolness of her forearm. Then his fingers. Then his palm.

She died that afternoon, but waited until Peter Michael had left the room.

Thirty-Eight

To keep Maryanne from seeing my grief that night, I went to Mom for comfort. She rocked in her chair while I sat on the bed. When the late afternoon darkened into nightfall, a full moon threw soft shadows into the corners of the room. We didn't bother to turn on the lamp. "I feel her presence so strongly," I said, wishing I were small enough to crawl onto mom's lap.

"She knows you're sad, Gloria. She's here tonight. With us. Just because you stop breathing doesn't necessarily mean you're gone. All that energy we keep building over all those years must live on somehow." She came over to the bed and sat down beside me. "At least for awhile." She smoothed my hair and patted my hand. "I've got an idea. Let's invite her to the wedding."

My heart sank. Mom's confusion had cleared after she moved in with us and became swept up by life again, but it seemed to be returning now. "What do you mean, Mom?" I asked, tearing a tissue from a box of Kleenex on her bedside table.

"There's an old Irish custom that if someone dies during the year before a wedding, an unmarried woman in the family makes a wreath of flowers from her garden and brings it to the wedding so the person's spirit knows where to sit. And since the wedding's going to be held in Brewster Gardens, I think flowers from that garden would be appropriate, don't you?"

"Where to sit?"

"Relax, Gloria. I don't mean 'pull up a chair and have a seat.' What I mean is that you invite the spirit and memory of them to join you." The sound of her low chuckle in the darkened room was comforting. "We could call Bradley and see if his girlfriend would be willing to do it. She's coming to the wedding with him and she might want to do something nice for his sister. Or do you think Apolonia would be willing to make a wreath? She's your friend, almost a member of our family. And her father was in the same nursing home with that lady, so that makes her more than just family. She's family on both sides of the aisle, sort of. Let's ask if she wants to do it."

Thirty-Nine

The day of the wedding was unseasonably warm for the end of September. Kevin borrowed Tony's gray three-piece suit. The arms were a little long and the sleeves had to be folded up an inch, but the pants were a perfect fit. Ida insisted on buying him a white shirt and a bow tie that looked suspiciously like a Monarch butterfly. "I'm dancing to my own drummer," she said, when anyone commented on the tie.

Vinny's twins wore matching ruby-colored princess costumes from Halloween, and Apolonia replaced the cone-shaped crowns with wreaths of small pink roses and baby's breath.

Steve, Frank's partner, borrowed Tony's truck to pick up the chairs early Sunday morning. Steve's father owned a funeral parlor, and since there were no wakes or funerals planned for Sunday he let us borrow fifty-one fold-up chairs. I drove over with Steve and waited in the parking lot by the entrance to the small embalming room. As he and his father loaded chairs into the truck, my curiosity got the best of me. I stepped inside.

A pink plastic container and tubing hung on the wall next to an anatomy chart. The stainless steel table and sink and the white tile walls were immaculate. I noticed two open boxes on the counter beneath closed cabinets. One contained eyeglasses and the other a haphazard pile of a dozen or so watches. Thinking of Ray, I began to pick through the watches, looking for a Waltham like his. "In the market for a pair of glasses?" Steve's father asked as he came back from the truck. "I donate them to the Lions Club if the family doesn't want them back."

I took Ray's Waltham watch from my purse and handed it to him. "Do you have any like this?" I asked.

"No, but I can fix this one," he said. "Give me a week."

Bradley and his girlfriend were still setting up the chairs when Kevin and Maryanne arrived. I placed the wreath that Apolonia had made on a chair at the end of the first row, next to where Mom would be sitting.

Two slim women in black dresses and a man in a black dinner tux sang music from the forties accappella as they strolled among the clusters of tourists who stopped to watch and the guests who began to take their seats. When Vinny, his Justice of the Peace license tucked into the pocket of his tweed jacket, stepped onto the bridge and turned to face us, there was a moment's hush. Kevin and Maryanne joined hands. Maryanne carried a stalk of white Amaryllis she had cut from the overgrown garden behind the bed and breakfast that morning. We stood and watched as they walked down the aisle behind the twins while the cabaret trio sang, *May I Have This Dance for The Rest of My Life.*

Tony wound his fingers through mine when they made their vows. Silently, we renewed our own. After Kevin placed the ring on Maryanne's finger and lifted her hand to his lips, she laid her other hand gently on his bowed head. Then she slipped her fingers beneath his chin and raised his face to kiss him. After they had been introduced for the first time as husband and wife, the trio sang *Joyful, Joyful We Adore Thee.* Both the guests and people who had stopped to watch joined in as they walked back up the aisle.

Mom brought the wreath to Maryanne. "What should we do with this?" she asked. "Should we put it in the stream so it can go out to sea?"

"No, nana, save it. We're going to put it above the bed in the master bedroom. I'm going to drape a lace canopy from it and use red ribbon tie-backs."

"Rose would be better," Mom said.

Forty

It wasn't quite low tide when we arrived at Long Beach for the reception. Several folding tables and chairs were arranged on the nearly deserted beach, covered with diaphanous white shawls that were anchored by baskets of fresh corn muffins, loaves of pumpernickel bread, and frosted pitchers of tea. Each table was decorated with clear glass bowls filled with fragrant beach roses, sea glass and seashells. On the sand close to the tables, clutches of white balloons were held in place by varnished beach stones. Frank directed the guests to large wicker baskets on the jetty and invited them to help themselves to kites, bubble pipes and Frisbees to pass the time while he and his crew finished preparing grilled Chilean sea bass, Caesar salad, and large bowls of honeydew melons, mangoes, and blueberries.

By the time the tide began to turn, the flaming cherries jubilee had been served and the balloons and kites had been released to the sky. Tables and chairs were folded and put in the back of Kevin's truck. The wind shifted and a cold breeze came off the ocean as the guests began to leave. Frank tucked shawls around both Ida and Mom's shoulders.

"All weddings are different," Ida said as Tony drove her, Mom and me home. "But I think this one was the best."

"Absolutely," Mom agreed.

Ida tapped me on the shoulder. "Do they know what it's going to be yet? A boy or a girl?"

"A girl."

"In that case, Ida," Mom said, "maybe we should write down a few ideas."

"Ideas?"

"Just in case we're not around for that particular wedding.

I'm not planning on living forever. Are you?"

"I've got a better idea," Ida said. "Why don't we just leave it up to Frank?"

"Absolutely. And I think Maryanne should pick out the wedding gown. What do you think?"

"Absolutely. She's got class." We drove the rest of the way home in silence, each of us reliving our own favorite part of the day and enjoying the cozy warmth of the car.

Forty-One

I had forgotten to write a final discharge note in Rose's chart until her brother called a few days later. He asked if I would mind keeping her belongings in my office until the weekend, when he could come pick them up.

"I'm doing okay," he said. "But I just can't go near that room right now. I thought it would be easier if Peter Michael and I just stopped by and saw you for a minute." I asked him how Peter Michael was doing and he chuckled. "He put the lucky stones in her casket, and now he wishes he had them back."

I jotted down Rose's brother's address and put it in my purse, planning to send a card to Peter Michael that night on my way home from work.

Forty-Two

Paul was still creating problems for Kathleen. His sister bought him a set of light blue scrubs for his birthday, and he talked a nurse's aide into giving him her nametag before she left on a maternity leave. He used art supplies stored in a desk in Kathleen's office to change the name to his own, then pinned the counterfeit tag on to his shirt.

The trouble started when Eric, the angry son of Otto Himmler, a resident with a diagnosis of morbid obesity, tried to force his way behind the nurses' station to look through his father's chart and find out why his new diet recommendations weren't being followed. Ruby paged me to intervene.

A vein pulsed on the side of the son's head. "I wanna see the damn chart," he shouted when he saw me coming down the hall.

"What's the problem?" I asked.

"I talked with his doctor, and he said my father should be getting super cereal every morning and double portions for lunch and supper. Why isn't he getting them? I wanna see the chart." Otto sat in a doublewide wheelchair behind Eric, nodding his head until his jowls shook as he emphasized each angry word that flew out of Eric's mouth.

"We never got any orders like that, Gloria," Ruby said as she pulled the chart from the rack.

"Gimme the chart!" Eric and Ruby struggled back and forth across the counter for possession of the chart.

Visitors stopped their conversations and residents glanced over at us. One elderly woman, sensing the potential for disaster, pushed her ancient mother's wheelchair down the hall and out of harm's way. I reached over the counter and rescued the chart. "Why don't the four of us go into the back room? We can look at it there. Together," I said.

We gathered around the table and Eric looked over Ruby's shoulder as she ran her finger down page after page.

Ruby closed the chart. "I don't know how there could have been new orders anyhow, since his doctor's been on vacation," she said. She raised her voice. "Who did you talk to, Mr. Himmler? What did the doctor look like?"

Otto looked at his son and pointed at his hearing aid.

Eric leaned over and shouted, "Dad, she wants to know what the doctor looked like." Otto looked puzzled, cupped his hand behind his ear and shook his head. Eric cupped both hands over his father's ear and tried again. As we all waited for a response, Otto shook his head again.

"Never mind," the son said to me. He slammed the chart closed and slid it across the table to Ruby. "Just straighten it out and call me. I've got to get back to work. I want this fixed before supper tonight or I'm going to the Big Boss and heads will roll."

After he left the room I lowered my voice and asked Ruby who the Big Boss was.

"The administrator," Otto grinned.

Then Judy received a letter from Elizabeth Murphy's daughter, Emily, complaining that the new doctor had prescribed ginkgo biloba for her mother and the nurses refused give it to her. Judy paged me to her office. "She sent a copy of this to the ombudsman," Judy said, handing me a letter that had obviously been scrawled in hasty anger.

I didn't know Elizabeth well. She was a tall, often befuddled-looking woman with a flickering smile, who wore layers of clothing. I often saw her in the library arranging and rearranging the *Readers Digest* books by color and the rest of the books by size. Pleasantly vague, she wandered through Churchill Lake, often attempting to nurture the less mobile residents by covering them and tucking in the bedding when they complained they were too hot as they struggled to reach their call bells. She removed covers and tidied up rooms, arranging clothing by color and not by ownership. Flashing call lights left in her wake charted her progress as she moved through the building offering comfort, solace and chaos.

I called the ombudsman, an independent volunteer who advocated for the residents and their families. She agreed to meet with Elizabeth, Emily, Judy and myself to discuss Emily's concerns. Elizabeth insisted that she couldn't remember the doctor's name but she saw him every day. Judy said that was a sure sign her progressive dementia was progressing, and promised that the physician's assistant who came in three times a week would reevaluate Elizabeth on his next visit.

A few days later Judy called Elizabeth's daughter and said that the physician's assistant had recommended a low dose of a new Alzheimer's drug that had just come on the market. Emily asked to speak to me, and Judy put the call on hold before transferring her. "Be careful," she warned. "She's in denial and very angry. Leave all the medical questions for nursing. Just give her a little TLC and try to figure out what all the fuss is about. Call me back after you talk to her."

Emily began her conversation with me by saying, "My mother does not have Alzheimer's. The doctor told us it was dementia."

I took her mother's chart from the rack at the nurses' station and opened it to the physician's orders section. I read her the diagnosis I found: dementia, Alzheimer's type. When I spoke to Judy later, I apologized for trespassing on medical turf, but she said not to worry. "You must have done a good job," she added, "because after she talked to you she called me back and said to go ahead with the new medicine."

Shortly after Elizabeth began taking the medicine, her memories returned in a flood. The result was disastrous. Elizabeth was horrified to learn she had been a resident at Churchill Lake for four years. "What happened to all those years? Where did they go?" she said. "Why can't I remember them?" Angry and agitated, she demanded to know who had brought her to Churchill Lake. When Ruby explained that it had been the doctor's decision but that Emily had driven her, Elizabeth went into her room and tore up the photos in an album that Emily had given her for Mother's Day. "She's not my daughter," she said, refusing to take the phone when the nurses called Emily to ask her to help calm Elizabeth down. Later that night Elizabeth, choking on her sobs, had to be held so the night supervisor could give her a sedative.

A few days later, I passed the library on my way in to work. Emily was standing in front of the shelves rearranging the books. As quickly as her memory had returned, it vanished again into the mist of her confusion.

In all the commotion over the Alzheimer drug's effect, Elizabeth's supposed prescription for ginko biloba was forgotten. But we thought of it again when Mr. Montgomery began receiving thank-you notes from resident's families praising Churchill Lake as a state-of-the-arts nursing home because of its new on-site doctor, who was available seven days a week to solve medical problems for residents *and* families. After paging Judy and me to his office one morning, he waved one of the letters in front of us. "Check it out," he said. "Who the hell is this guy?"

"No one *we* know," Judy said.

The mystery was solved a few days later, when Apolonia brought her father homemade chicken soup because he said he couldn't eat the food in the dining room because the portions were too large and the food was too salty. "I want to file a formal complaint," she told me.

"What's wrong?" I asked.

"The activities director is on a power trip down in the gift shop.

She's trying to fire one of your doctors. She's completely out of control, and in my clinical opinion I think she's in the middle of a nervous breakdown. She's over the bend, Gloria. I knew she had a problem from that first meeting we had. There's always been something about her that didn't quite click with me."

"I like her," her father said.

"I know, Dad, I know."

Long before I reached the gift shop I could hear Kathleen screaming, "This is the last straw. You're fired! Get out." Judy, Maxine, and Mr. Montgomery were huddled together outside the door, discussing how to intervene without adding fuel to the fire. When they saw me coming Maxine stepped back. "It's all yours, kid," she said.

"Lower the volume, solve the problem and you've got tomorrow off," Mr. Montgomery said. "With pay." He walked back to his office and shut the door.

I went into the gift shop to find Paul sitting on a high stool behind the small counter, his crossed arms resting on his chest and his hands anchored in his armpits. He wore an expression of serene interest. The more agitated Kathleen became, the calmer he grew. "You're out of here," she shouted. Her belt came loose in her hand, and she wound it around her fist.

Judy reached in to the gift shop and pulled Kathleen gently away from the counter. "Come on, honey," she whispered. "I keep a bottle of scotch in my office downstairs."

I waved Maxine away, shut the door, and turned the 'open' sign around to 'closed.'

"Okay, Paul what's the problem?" I asked.

Paul shrugged, "I don't know. She just went psycho on me. You saw her."

"Why did she go psycho?"

"I don't know. All's I did was tell her she should see the shrink when he comes in on Wednesday. She doesn't have to worry because I broke the ice for her. I've already talked to him. I explained to her, calmly, that there's nothing to be ashamed of because every once in awhile we all need a little help and therapy is really something nice we do for ourselves." He glanced at the wall clock and then at his watch. "She needs a little something to take the edge off."

"You told her that?"

"Yes."

"When?"

"After we had our little discussion about my name tag."

"What do you mean?"

"She doesn't want me wearing a name tag."

"But you're not an employee, Paul. You're one of the residents. You *shouldn't* wear a name tag."

"That's true. That's true," he said, holding up his hand and nodding before anchoring his hand back under his armpit. "But it looks more professional when I'm working. I don't know how many times I've tried to explain that to her. She just doesn't get it."

The door behind us opened, a gray-haired woman with a large black standard poodle on a leash leaned in. "Excuse me, doctor, but we had an appointment." She tapped her watch.

"The doctor's not going to be able to see you today," I said closing the door. I opened my hand and held it out to Paul. Our eyes met and held for a long moment. "Give it to me, Paul," I said.

Reluctantly he undid the nametag and then dropped it on to my palm. "I guess you don't get it either," he said. "Oh well The Lord giveth and the Lord taketh away."

Forty-Three

"**Here's another one for** ya," Maxine said, as we shared her sub sandwich and I updated them on my meeting with Paul. "Physician, heal thyself. Try that one on 'im and see how he likes it."

Judy and Mr. Montgomery passed a cigarette back and forth while Kathleen slouched on the couch between them.

"Why is he still here?" Judy asked. "He doesn't have any skilled nursing needs and he's not getting therapy."

"How many empty beds do we have?" Mr. Montgomery asked.

"Shoot, if that's all that's keeping him here get him out and I'll throw myself in his bed," Kathleen said.

"*You're* the discharge planner," Judy said to me. All heads turned in my direction.

"Isn't a discharge supposed to be a team decision?" I asked.

Mr. Montgomery stubbed out the cigarette and said, "Okay, team, all in favor of discharge say 'aye.'"

We all said 'aye.' Mr. Montgomery stood up. "Gloria, do your stuff," he said, "Start the paperwork. Kathleen, you go home and sleep it off. Judy, why don't you drive her home and leave her car here? I'll figure out how to get it back to her later. Right now I just want to go into my office, close the door and stare at the wall for a couple of hours."

"That's okay," Maxine said, rubbing grease from her chin, crumbling the wrapping paper from the sandwich into a tight ball and slam dunking it into the wastebasket. "I'll give her a lift home. She can sleep in my car while I stop by the hospital to get a refill for the bed."

Forty-Four

Apolonia called me the night before Halloween. "I'm taking some kids out trick-or-treating tomorrow night. They've never been trick-or-treating before in their entire lives. Can you believe it? They don't even know what Halloween is. They asked me if it was like *Nightmare on Elm Street.* He's ten and his sister's eight and she's the one that asked me if Freddy Krueger would be there. I feel so bad for these kids," Apolonia said. "Why don't you come along? It should be fun."

I had always loved trick-or-treating with Maryanne and Bradley when they were small. For years, after they felt they were too grown up to dress up, I suffered a terrible sense of loss each Halloween night when we all sat at home. Then even the doorbell stopped ringing because trick-or-treating had become genuinely scary to adults fearing poisoned apples and razor blades. "Where should I meet you?" I asked.

"In front of the wax museum. We'll start out there and go trick-or-treating afterwards."

The next night, as I waited for Apolonia on a cold granite bench in front of the museum, I looked down the steep hill at the occasional groups of revelers on the sidewalk and realized they were all either teenagers or adults. Overcome by a wave of nostalgia, I watched Apolonia park her car and lift a sleeping baby dressed as Winnie the Pooh in to a backpack. She looked up and down the street. I called to her, but she didn't hear me.

"I'm up here, Apolonia," I called again, stepping to the top of the long flight of stairs that led down to the street. She still didn't seem to hear as she scanned the faces in a group of people passing by. Finally she reached into the car again and helped a little girl dressed as a ballerina and a boy dressed as a ghost on to the sidewalk. Holding their hands, she began to lead them up the stairs. When the little boy stumbled on the hem of his costume, holding his arm out stiffly by his side for balance, Apolonia stopped and adjusted his costume. Finally, she looked up and saw me at the top of the steps. When I waved, the children seemed to hang back.

"If they're scared to death of me," I whispered to Apolonia as we stood in line waiting to buy our tickets, "what are they going to do when they get inside the museum?"

"They'll love it."

"Have you ever been in this place before?"

"No."

"I have. I took Maryanne here when she was about twelve and she freaked out."

The little boy laughed and the little girl giggled.

"That was Maryanne. Whole different story here. Right kids?" Apolonia said, swinging their hands.

"Right," they said in unison.

"Gloria, this is Henry and this is Greta."

I held out my hand and Henry slapped it. Hard. "For crissakes," he said, "Let's *go*."

We joined a kindergarten outing from a local church whose rule was to take turns standing up front at each dimly lit scene. The rule for our small group was "elbows first."

"Am I wrong," Apolonia whispered, "or does that mannequin look like Elizabeth Taylor?"

"I think you're right," I said.

The midget ghouls and goblins pressing in close around us saw a small realistic cat curled up asleep under the table.

A little girl dressed as a bearded pirate said, "How did they get that cat to thtay tho thill?"

"Because he's dead," Greta said in a flat dull voice.

The pirate's eyes widened as Greta, our ballerina, tapped her with her wand and said, "They're dead and they're stuffed."

"No, honey, they're not dead," Apolonia said. "Gloria and I just saw a mannequin of a movie actress, and she's not dead and stuffed."

"Maybe she is. That cat is." Greta stuck her wand through the railing in front of the exhibit and upended the cat so that it was lying on its back with its feet in the air. "See?" she said. "Dead."

"No," Apolonia, said firmly. "That cat - "

"Skip it," I said, "Don't argue. Just ignore her and let's get out of here."

The adults in the church group herded their children from exhibit to exhibit, but as quickly as they moved they were unable to escape. Henry and Greta honed in on them like heat sensors, drawn to their despairing howls. Dead cats seemed to proliferate. They were everywhere. On chairs. In trees. Under tables. In piles of straw.

"It's endless," Apolonia said. "How many exhibits are there in this place?"

"Twenty-six," someone said in the dark. "And it empties out into a gift shop with a lot of breakable stuff."

"Holy shit," Greta said. "Can we go there?"

By the time we reached the exhibit of the Pilgrims burying their dead, Henry and Greta had absorbed the essence of Halloween and were reveling in their power to terrorize the others, adults and children alike. "And the dead guy all wrapped up like that is stuffed, too."

The church chaperones barely had time to cover as many ears as possible before Greta said, "And they're gonna put dirt all over him and it'll get in his nose and his mouth and his eyes... and he won't be able to breath or claw his way out 'cause they'll stamp down the dirt and hit him with a shovel."

Apolonia grabbed their hands, and the church group cowered against the walls submissively to let us pass. We were well ahead of them and would have made it out safely if Henry hadn't run ahead and pushed a button by the exhibit of the first landing. Suddenly the exhibit filled with lightning, rain and thunder. Our children climbed over the railing and splashed around, trying to catch rain on their tongues, as the church group arrived. Their children followed, slipping and sliding over each other and the rock, trying to hold each other up while screaming with laughter as they tumbled into the rocking, bottomless boat.

Forty-Five

"I hate this job," Apolonia said, strapping the sleeping baby into its car seat and fastening the seat belts around the two soaking children.

"That was *great*," Henry said, holding out a hand full of quarters.

"Where'd you get those?" Apolonia asked.

"In the water."

"I got some, too," Greta said, holding out her hand.

"Yeah, but yours are just pennies," the little boy said. The girl punched him and he punched her back then pulled her hair.

"Should I make them take it back tonight?" Apolonia said, pulling them away from each other as coins flew all over the back seat, joining two empty Happy Meal bags and several discarded candy wrappers.

"I'm too tired," I said. "Let's do it tomorrow."

"The best part for me was the part about the dead cats and the kid with the fake moustache," Greta said. "Was that a boy or a girl, Apolonia?"

Before Apolonia could answer the little boy said, "Can we do it again tomorrow?"

"No," she said.

"You said we could," he said.

"No, I didn't."

"Yes you did."

The little girl undid her seat belt and tried to crawl up front with Apolonia and put her arm around her neck. "When can we go back?"

"Never. Sit down and put that seat belt back on or I'm going to lose my mind."

They began to swing their feet and kick the back of our seats with such force that I began rocking back and forth. "We wanna go back, we wanna go back," they sang over and over until the baby woke up and began to whine. Greta fished a baby bottle out of the bag on the floor and passed it to the baby who threw it up front, where it hit the windshield, rolled off the dashboard, and fell to the floor and under the brake pedal.

"We want to go back. We want to go back," they chanted as I undid my seat belt and retrieved the bottle.

"Not in this lifetime, kids," Apolonia said, "And if there is such a thing as reincarnation, I'm not coming back if I have to do this again."

We had been driving long enough for the soft thrum of the engine to lull the children asleep. I dozed off too, but when the car swerved I was suddenly fully awake. "What is it?" I asked. "Is everything all right?" Apolonia smoothed her hair behind her ear as she glanced from the rearview mirror to the side mirror. "Where are we?" I said, unable to read the signs on the side of the dark road as we hurtled by them. "Are we lost?"

Apolonia bit at her lower lip. "No."

"We're over the speed limit, aren't we?" She looked from the road to the rear view mirror and didn't say anything but slowed the car to slightly above the speed limit.

"What's wrong?" The children were asleep, their mouths open and their heads resting on each other's shoulders. The baby's car seat was next to the window. He was studying his reflection in the dark glass, his thumb tucked into the corner of his mouth.

"I lied to you," Apolonia finally said.

"About what?"

"Are they asleep?"

I looked back again. The baby turned from the window and

gave me a sleepy smile. "Everyone but the baby. What's up, Apolonia? After all we've been through together tonight I think I have the right to know." Even gentle teasing didn't break the silence between us. I put my head back and closed my eyes.

"I'm afraid," she said softly. In the glow of the dashboard lights I could see the lines of worry around her eyes. "I asked you to come along tonight because I'm scared."

"Of what?" She turned and looked at me for a brief moment before checking the rear view mirror and then concentrating on the road. "It has something to do with the kids, doesn't it?" I said.

"You're always so calm - " she began.

"Me!"

"Yes, you. You know what you're doing. You roll with the punches. Look at all that's happened just since we graduated, and no matter what cards life deals you you reshuffle them and play them out to win. You're unflappable."

"You must mean inscrutable, because that's certainly not how I feel. Not at all."

She took my hand and squeezed it quickly; "I've seen you in operation, Gloria, not just in your life but at work too. No matter what comes up or what's going on around you you keep calm. I need someone calm around me tonight because I'm scared to death."

"Where are we taking these kids?"

"Their mother's waiting for them in a house in Acton. As soon as I drop them off someone will drive them to a safe house."

"Apolonia, this is crazy. She's always gone back to him before. Why are you putting yourself at risk like this? For what?"

"She always went back because he found her. We told her

that if she backs out this time she loses the kids. He won't find her this time."

I looked into the side mirror outside my window. "There's a car behind us."

"I know. I see him," she said, pressing down on the gas pedal. The car sped up and then swerved around us. The woman driving the car gave us the finger. It looked like she was swearing at Apolonia.

We pulled off the highway and onto a series of roads that curved and dipped through dark woods and past moonlit fields. Eventually we came to a house at the end of a tree-lined one-way street.

Apolonia pulled into the circular driveway and parked the car behind a high cluster of bushes. We sat in the car until the side door opened and a narrow shaft of light fell across the small porch. Apolonia turned off the car lights and a woman beckoned towards us.

"That's my boss," Apolonia said, "She's walking me through this. The house belongs to a volunteer who's going to drive them to the safe house as soon as we leave."

"Let me guess," I said. "In case he was following, he'll keep following us, and that'll give them a chance to get away."

The children began to stir in the seat behind us.

"Are you mad at me?" Apolonia asked.

"Mad at you! Talk about understatements!"

The door opened wider and the woman beckoned to us again. "Well, here goes," Apolonia said to me. "You take the baby. Don't bother with the car seat; they've got one."

Greta started to get out of the car, but Henry pulled her back. "Come on, come on," Apolonia said, trying to lift her out of the car. She clung to her brother, scratching and crying. Henry kicked and swore pulling, at Apolonia's arms as he tried to free his sister.

Another woman had come to the door. I took a chance and said, in the firm voice that had worked so well with Maryanne and Bradley when they were children, "Kids, look." I took advantage of a moment of shocked silence to say, "There's your mom." They pushed their way out of the car and ran towards the porch.

Apolonia popped the lid to the trunk and hurried after the children. "Bring those bags in," she called back over her shoulder. I took out several grocery bags filled with clothes, slammed down the lid of the trunk, and looked around the dark yard and the pine trees that edged the property. The wind had picked up and sounded like stormy ocean surf. I gasped when I noticed movement in the back yard, but it was only a swaying tire at the end of a rope hanging from the branch of an apple tree.

Inside the front hall one of the bags I was holding burst open and clothes and toys scattered across the floor. Apolonia knelt beside me to help gather them up and then sat back on her heels and held up what was left of the Wild Woman apron she had bought at the Waterfront Fair. The apron had been slashed to ribbons. "Hide this," she whispered. "He cut it up during one of their fights." When I didn't move she gave me a shove and said, "Quick, get rid of it."

I stumbled out to the car and tossed the apron into the back seat. The wind gusted through the bushes behind me. I slid back inside, slamming the door and clawing at the locks until they were all secured. Heavy rain tattooed on the roof of the car. I saw Apolonia, the car keys in her hand, running towards me, and opened the door. She threw herself inside and jabbed the keys toward the ignition until I grabbed them from her and shoved the key in place. We began to back out of the driveway, the driver's side door swinging out and slapping the bushes. "Shut the door. Shut the door and lock it," I screamed, leaning over Apolonia and nearly falling out as I struggled to reach the handle. She pushed me away, shut the door and skidded onto the road, facing the wrong direction.

"This is a one-way street," I shouted. "Turn around!"

"After a night like tonight you're going to worry about going the wrong way on a deserted one-way street?" But she spun the car around until we were, at last, facing away from the house at the end of the street and on our way home.

Mom was asleep and Tony was alone sitting on the coach in the living room with a bowl of candy on the floor beside him. When he saw me come in the front door he clicked off the sound on the television. "Where were you?" he said.

"Did anyone come to the house?"

"No. Not one kid. I thought you and Apolonia would at least bring those kids over after you finished up at the museum. You always buy too much candy and then we're stuck with it afterwards."

Suddenly my legs felt as though all the strength had left them. I held onto the doorway for support. He came over and put his arms around me. "What's wrong?" he said. "What happened?"

I told him about the museum and the ride to Acton. "And then on the way home," I said, "she got pulled over for speeding. No matter how she tried to explain why she was speeding it didn't matter. He just didn't give a damn, Tony. He just kept on taking his time, writing the ticket as slowly as he could, sitting in the cruiser and trying to look busy. Stalling, stalling, stalling and ma'am-ing her to death. 'Yes, ma'am' this and 'no ma'am' that. And when I tried to say something he bent down, looked in the car and said, 'Did you say something?' in this cold-as-ice voice. It was a threat, Tony. It was definitely a threat. I took down his badge number, and I'm going to find out his boss's name."

"He might have saved your life."

"Saved my life! Don't you humor me. Don't side with him. He was a no good fascist son of a bitch with small-man syndrome. I wanted to kill him." I pushed Tony aside, took a step away from him and nearly fell. We were both shocked by the depth of my rage, but Tony recovered first and put his arms around me again. I put my head against his shoulder and sobbed. "I was so afraid," I finally said. "I thought for sure when we were sitting on the side of the road waiting for him to finish writing that ticket we were going to be gunned down by that woman's husband."

"Where's Apolonia now?"

I checked my watch. "On her way home. I tried to get her to stay over but she insisted on going home. She carries Mace in her pocketbook, Tony, and keeps a baseball bat beside her bed. What a way to live."

Tony said he thought the baseball bat was a bad idea because if anyone broke into the house they would probably wrestle the bat away and use it on her. He also volunteered to install motion-sensitive lights on the outside of the house. "Give her a few more minutes and then call and make sure she got home all right. And, babe?" he said, picking up the bowl of candy, "I'm sorry I was so angry at you when you first got home. I was just worried when it got so late and you weren't back yet."

"*You* were angry? I didn't even notice. I thought *I* was the one that was angry."

I called Apolonia and tried again to convince her to spend the night with us. She refused, but she did accept Tony's suggestion about the lights for the house.

Tony reassured me that no one had followed us home, and that if we had been followed, talking to a state trooper might have been a good thing. "The contact with a cop - "

"Even if he's a ticket-writing fascist?"

"Even if he's a ticket-writing fascist, would be good, because someone driving by wouldn't know what you were talking about and it would probably scare him off."

Exhausted I went upstairs, got ready for bed and crawled between the covers while Tony shut down the house. It was comforting to hear him downstairs moving from room to room, lowering the blinds and checking the locks on all the doors before moving quietly through his nightly ritual of removing his watch and wallet, putting them on top of the dresser, undressing and putting on his pajama bottoms. Then he carried his clothes over to the chair near the window and tossed them on the seat. Halfway to the bed, he paused for a moment then crossed back toward the chair. At first I thought he was going to retrieve something from the pocket of his trousers, but instead he pulled back the curtain and stood for a long time looking down at the yard outside the house. That was not part of his nightly ritual.

Forty-Six

It took a long time to get to sleep that night. When I did, the dream was waiting for me. The massive white bear lumbered on to the horizon. I tried to warn Mom, who stood blissfully unaware of the peril closing in on her. She stood smiling, barefooted on the ice, her white nightgown billowing gently around her. I strained forward trying to get on to the ice to save her, but was immobilized by an unseen force.

Each time I drifted off to sleep the dream came back. Each time stronger and more real. And each time my throat felt raw, as though I had been calling out for help, but Tony was sleeping peacefully at my side. Finally, I took a blanket and a pillow into Mom's room and spent the rest of the night sitting in her rocker, comforted by the gentle rise and fall of her chest as she slept.

Forty-Seven

Early Saturday morning Ruby called and asked me to come in. "It's an emergency," she said.

I squinted at the bedside clock. "Ruby, it's eight o'clock. It's a Saturday. I'm not even out of bed yet."

"The fractured pelvis is getting ready to walk. You've got to come in and talk to him."

When the fractured pelvis' company downsized he had been forced into an early retirement. After the novelty of sleeping in and watching television wore off, he began filling his empty hours by tackling small jobs around the house to ward off boredom. One Saturday he cleaned out gutters while his wife shopped. She didn't see him when she got home, so she put the groceries away and went off to an afternoon Mass. After Mass, in the middle of preparing supper, she rinsed off her hands and happened to look out the kitchen window above the sink. The ladder was still up. She went outside to put it away and found her husband lying on the ground where he had spent three hours passing in and out of consciousness. He was airlifted to a Boston hospital where steel rods were inserted into his fractured pelvis and then came to Churchill Lake for rehab.

"Can it wait until this afternoon? I promised a friend I'd help her buy a dog this morning."

"It can't wait. I already told him you'd be in and made him promise not to leave until you had a chance to talk to him."

By now I was fully awake and sitting up in bed with one arm wrapped around my knees. "How does he plan to get home?"

"He talked his wife into coming in and picking him up. I talked to her, too. She's not happy about the whole thing but she's coming in."

"Why is it all of the sudden a crisis? I was there yesterday and he seemed okay."

"The therapists told him they weren't going to discharge him till next Friday because he needed an extra week. He brooded about it all night. They had to bring him out to the nurse's station because he couldn't sleep and wouldn't take anything to help him sleep. Now he's all worked up because he thinks we're going to keep him here forever. The nurse's aide is in there with him now because he's wandering around on his walker and packing up his things. I'm afraid he's going to fall, and I don't want to even think where those steel rods will wind up. Nobody can reason with him. You've got to do something, Gloria. All the other residents are beginning to rev up."

I swung my legs over the side of the bed and began taking clothes out of the drawers and closet while we talked. "Stall him. Call his wife and tell her not to come in until I get there and have a chance to talk to him."

By the time I'd finished my shower and came downstairs, Mom and Tony were sitting at the kitchen table drinking coffee and sharing the morning paper. I explained my change in plans to them and then I called Apolonia and told her I'd pick her up when I got back from Churchill Lake. "Great," she said. "That gives me a chance to clear up some paperwork at the office."

"Tony's coming over this morning to put up the lights."

"I remember. I gave you the extra key to the house, right?"

"Right."

"I'll leave some iced tea in the fridge for him."

I drove to the end of the street and kept picturing Tony up on a ladder. Alone. I took four right turns and pulled to the curb in front of the house just as he was crossing the street and heading back to the house from his truck.

"Just loading up," he said. "Did you forget something?"

"We've got to talk," I said, walking beside him as I gave him a thumbnail sketch of where I was going and why. "I'd feel safer if there was someone there while you're up on a ladder," I said.

"Like who?" Tony checked his tool belt.

"Mom."

"Mom? She'd be a big help." Mom put the newspaper aside and looked up. "No offense, Mom, but what could you do if something happened?"

"Call 911," she said.

"Gloria, that was him and this is me. I walked high-rise steel, for crissakes."

"That was before you knew me," I said.

"That guy probably didn't know a ball-peen hammer from a jackhammer."

"That's dangerous," Mom said. "I was married to one of those."

"I'm not going to argue with you about this, Tony," I said. "Mom, go with him and just keep an eye on him in case anything happens." I gave her my cell phone and the key to the house, "Check on him once in a while and make sure he's okay. And if he's not - "

"Call 911," she said.

"What could possibly go wrong?" Tony asked as he gathered up his tools and I helped him load the ladder on the back of his pickup. I ran though a litany of possible disastrous scenarios until he stopped me. "Gloria," he said, "I'll be fine. Mom doesn't have to go with me, but if it'll make you feel better it's okay with me. She can bring a book and a fold-up chair and work on her tan." He pulled some bills from his wallet and said, "Take Apolonia to lunch when you get back."

"And stay out of your hair?"
"I didn't say that."
"I read your mind."

Forty-Eight

The skirmish with Tony prepared me for my meeting with the fractured pelvis. He was fully dressed, his belongings were piled on his bed and he was sitting by the window looking out at the parking lot. The nurse's aide gave me a grateful smile and left the room as soon as I came in. I put my pocketbook on the bed, opened his wheelchair and pulled it over closer to him and sat down. "Where are you going?" I asked.

"Home."

"How are you going to get there?"

"I'm waiting for my wife." He glanced at his watch. "She should have been here by now. What are you doing in here? It's Saturday."

"They called and asked me to come in."

"I'm sorry they put you though all that trouble for nothing, because it's not going to make any difference. I'm going home." He looked out the window again.

I reached over and rested my hand on his arm, "Tell me what happened between the time I saw you on Friday and today." He rubbed his finger over his eyebrow. "Hum?"

He looked back out the window and finally said, "They're not going to let me go. I'm stuck here. I should have gone right home from the hospital."

"They only want you to stay an extra week."

He turned on me quickly, and then winced. "That's what they say, but it's not what they mean. Nobody's being upfront with me. Nobody tells me the truth."

"I thought you trusted me."

"I did." Although he had raised his voice, he hadn't moved his arm.

"Going into a nursing home isn't like stepping in to

quicksand," I said. "It's not as if you're trapped." A faint trace of a fleeting smile told me I was on the right path. "You know how you winced just now?" He turned carefully in my direction, "It was because you moved too quickly. They only want you to stay until next Friday." He glanced back at the window and almost pulled his arm away. "I'm going to go out right now and get discharge papers for you to sign today. Then on Monday, you'll come to my office and together we'll set up all the services you'll need at home; a nurse, a home health aide, therapists."

I went down to my office and began the paperwork for him to sign. I told Ruby what I was doing. "He doesn't have a discharge order yet," she said.

"Are they definitely planning on Friday?"

"Yes."

"Then get the order."

After he signed his discharge papers, he asked me to clear off his bed because he wanted to lie down. He pushed the call light for a nursing assistant. "Could you call my wife and tell her not to come in till this evening?" he asked. "I want to take a nap."

Forty-Nine

The lights had been installed and Apolonia was helping Tony reload his pickup by the time I got to her house. "Look at you," she said, "You're glowing. What happened?"

"Today I really truly feel like I belong at Churchill Lake," I said. "When no one else could convince a resident to stay I did it. I told Ruby to 'do this,' and she did it." I felt the blossom of revelation and power open slowly in my chest. "People listen to me." I hugged Tony. "I'm a social worker."

"Oh, yeah?" Apolonia said. "You're a social worker because people listen to you? Then what am I?" She thanked Tony for putting up the lights, and he and Mom agreed to stay until we got home. "Come on, Girl Wonder," she said, "Put on your cape and let's go get me a man-eating dog."

Fifty

I pulled out Frank's directions to the pound where he had bought a golden retriever, a big, friendly dog that walked with a limp and always kept an eager eye on Frank, waiting to be told what to do next.

"Actually, he said he 'rescued' his dog from this place and that we should 'be prepared,' whatever that means," I told Apolonia. "He used to bring it to the bed and breakfast when he was helping Maryanne set up the kitchen. That dog would just curl up in the corner and wait to be told where to go or what to do. That's the kind of dog you need. Something that's completely devoted to you."

"I prefer cats."

"Cats don't bark."

"But they sit in the window and wait for you to get home and you can leave them alone for a week with a box of kitty litter, a bowl of water, and a roasting pan filled with cat food."

"If this guy shows up, you need something that will frighten him away, something big and vicious whose bite's worse than his bark."

"And a whip and chain to keep it under control? No, what I need," she said, "is a new life." She slowed the car and said, "You're not afraid of dogs, are you?" I shook my head. "Then there's no way you can understand how I feel right now. I'm terrified."

"Oh yes I can," I said. "I use to be terrified of dogs, too, until I took this job." She shot me a puzzled look. "Yeah," I said.

"So?"

"So there's a woman who brings in a massive German shepherd to visit her dad, and if it's on the same day that the guy with the pit bull brings his dog into visit his mom the nurse's aides call me to break up the fights."

"You're kidding."

"No. The first time it happened I was terrified. The second time I asked them to keep the dogs separated on the patio during visits. And the next time I was so angry I didn't even realize I had pulled the dogs apart until it was all over. The thing you have to keep in mind and never forget is that with dogs you have to show them who's the alpha male. One of the residents who used to raise dogs told me that all dogs are descended from wolves, and they only obey the leader of the pack."

Apolonia looked at me from the corner of her eye and said, "What are you talking about? You have to break up dogfights? Was that in your job description?"

"I didn't know what this job was going to be like when I signed on. But I'll tell you this, it's sure not like watching the grass grow."

By the time we reached the dog pound, a grouping of kennels and sheds on the edge of a large pig farm, I had convinced Apolonia that a homeless waif would be so grateful to have a place of its own that he would look upon her as his savior and attach his fangs to the neck of anyone who threatened her.

The man who ran the pound came out of the farmhouse as we were parking the car and stood on the porch with his fists on his hips. He was tall and wiry, with a pronounced Adam's apple and hollow cheeks. He wore a sweat-stained John Deere baseball cap, torn jeans, a plaid shirt, and heavy black leather boots. "I'm scared to death of dogs," she said, "but I think I can do this."

"Sure you can." I opened the car door and stepped into a muddy puddle deep enough that the water poured in over the top of my shoe.

The man stepped down off the steps and began leading us to the kennels. I noticed a pronounced hitch in his gait. "He's got sciatica," I said.

"How do you know?"

"When you work in a nursing home you just know these things."

Apolonia's three-inch heels stuck in the muddy path leading down to the shabby kennels. She took my arm to steady herself while pulling her foot free and calling out after his retreating back, "I can see why you wear boots."

He looked over his shoulder and grunted but didn't slow his pace.

"Don't tell him why you want the dog," I whispered.

"Why?" she whispered back.

"He's scary. He looks like he could be a stalker himself."

"Then let's ask him what dog would scare him and have him wrap it up."

In the first kennel, a thin, twitching dog paced back and forth shooting nervous glances in our direction as we approached. "What are those sores all over his legs?" I asked. As if on cue the dog collapsed and began to ferociously burrow his long thin snout into one of the raw wounds on his rear leg. "Stop that!" Apolonia, shouted, "Stop that!" She hit her pocketbook against the front of the cage, dragging it back and forth until the dog sprang up and mashed its muzzle against the wire door, barking and salivating, gnawing on the cage as it tried to bite its way through to Apolonia. She clutched her pocketbook to her chest and stepped back, grinding her heel into the man's shoe. "I'm sorry," she said spinning around to face him. "I'm so sorry. Did I hurt you?" She reached out and almost touched his arm. He hadn't moved, which forced her to step backwards till her back was almost against the snarling dog's cage.

He tipped his baseball cap with a grin and, in a voice that was pure gravel said, "That's okay, little lady. These are shit-kicker boots. Ya couldn't hurt me even if ya tried."

The next dog, a large-eyed, sweet-faced animal, saw us coming and scurried from the far corner of its cage to make intense eye contact with Apolonia. The closer she got to the dog the faster its small pink tongue lapped the wire door of the cage. "This one looks harmless," Apolonia said. "I don't think I'd have to be afraid of him." She put her hand and then her face against the wire and allowed the tongue to lap her cheek. The man looked on with an expression of disgust as she said, "Oh, what a sweet liddle grateful baby. How did a liddle grateful sweetums like you wind up in a scary ole place like this?"

"Someone dumped that in the woods," the man said. "It's been living wild for awhile."

"Isn't that a French bull dog?" I asked.

"Yeah."

"Don't they usually cost over a thousand dollars?"

"Yeah. So? What's your point?"

The dog began to wriggle and make soft whimpering noises in response to Apolonia's soothing coos and kisses. "They cost more than what my daughter paid for her first car. Why would someone abandon a dog like that?"

The dog stood up on its quivering hind legs, twitching with excitement, still lapping the wire door and began to urinate on Apolonia. She pulled a wad of Kleenex from her pocketbook and began to brush off her blouse, "Got anything else?" she asked.

"What are you looking for?" the man asked. "Company or cop?"

Apolonia and I exchanged a brief glance and I said, "Let's see a little of both."

"Only got two more dogs. They're not much, but I'll be getting more in by the end of the week if you want to come back then."

"Can we see them?" I asked.

He reluctantly led us to a large cage separated from the others. Beyond the cage, a medium-sized dog tethered to a stake in the ground stared at us as he pranced continuously in a circular rut at least four inches deep. Patches of his reddish brown fur seemed to be missing along his bony ribcage. His pointed ears twitched and his tongue lolled from one side of his mouth to the other. With each circle he completed he would momentarily look away from us as he lunged unsuccessfully at a water dish just beyond his reach. Then the pacing would begin again.

"Is that a German shepherd?" Apolonia asked.

"Nah. He's a mixed nothing. Might be part fox. Look at the tail."

"Look at this one," Apolonia said, going up to the isolated cage, "he looks like the dog in the Body Snatchers. Remember that film, Gloria? The dog with the human face?" The dog tilted its head from side to side, watching Apolonia closely as I went over to the dog on the end of the chain and moved the water dish closer to him. "What's this dog's name?" she asked.

"Dead Dog," the man said. He leaned over Apolonia's shoulder and punched the side of the cage. The dog's menacing growl rattled in its throat as his lips pulled back over his teeth.

"Gloria," Apolonia called out. "Come look at this. This dog's got human teeth and fangs! What kind of a dog is this?"

"A pit bull," the man said. "Chewed someone up. Pit bulls don't bite. They eat." He put his face close to the cage and lowered his voice. "Going down tomorrow, aren't ya, Dead Dog? Dead Dog walking." He smashed his fist against the cage with such force that the cage trembled. The dog struggled to regain its footing, then lunged at him.

Apolonia came over to where I crouched by the other dog as he lapped up the last of the water in the bowl and let me scratch his ears. "Let's get out of here," she said softly.

"How much for this dog?" I asked.

The man came over and kicked the water bowl away. The dog stumbled in and out of the rut, barking and lunging at the man's black boots as he walked back and forth, teasing the dog. "Come on, come on," he said. "You want me? Get me!"

"How much for the dog?" I asked again. Louder this time.

"Fifty bucks," he shouted over the dog's frantic barking.

"We're not interested," Apolonia said, taking my arm and pulling me to my feet.

"Yes, we are." I gave him thirty dollars. Reluctantly, Apolonia gave me another twenty. "I'm not giving you a penny for any of these dogs," she said to him, "but I'll give it to my friend."

"Doesn't matter to me," the man smiled, counting out the bills and stuffing them into his pocket. "Money's money."

Getting the dog into the back seat of the car was the hardest part of the drive. Once he was inside and the door was shut, he paced back and forth on the seat, pulling himself up on his front paws to look out the back window and bark. Then he fell to the floor, crawled up on the seat and repeated the cycle until we turned the corner of the road. After the ramshackle farm and the sheds and kennels behind it disappeared from sight, the dog fell over, righted himself, and looked out the back window again, this time resting his chin between his paws. First one pert ear would twitch and then the other. Occasionally, he turned his head and looked at us.

Apolonia glanced at him in the rearview mirror. "He looks

like he's got eyebrows," she said.

"Dogs don't have eyebrows."

"That dog does. Look at him."

I turned in the seat and looked back at the dog. He stared at me for a moment and then the skin above one eye rippled upward. "See that?" Apolonia said, "That's an eyebrow."

"That's a twitch."

By the time we got home he was sound asleep, stretched out on the back seat of the car with his chin resting on his paws. Tony attached a length of clothesline to his neck, woke him up, and led him in to the back yard, where he bathed him using Apolonia's herbal shampoo and a large sponge she kept under the sink for washing windows. Mom arranged a nest of blankets in the living room and spread out newspaper in the bathroom.

When the dog came into the house, Tony untied the clothesline. The dog leapt on to a chair and began barking and then rushed across the living room floor and slid to a stop in front of Mom. He stretched his front paws out, lowered his head, and continued to bark at her shoes, lunging forward and then cowering away. "The floor shakes when he barks," Mom said, as she scrambled up on top of the sofa.

"Kick off your shoes," I said. "He doesn't like your shoes, Mom."

"Well, neither do I," she shouted, toeing off her black orthopedic shoes and kicking them on to the floor. While the first was in mid-air, the dog jumped up and snatched it into his mouth and swung the shoe from side to side, hitting it repeatedly against the sofa. Finally, he dragged it across the floor and stuffed it under a bookcase with his nose and paw. Mom tucked the other shoe under the sofa cushion and sat down. The dog walked over slowly, licked her feet, and then lay down beside her and rested his chin on his paws. His ears twitched and he looked up at her, twitching first one eyebrow and then the other.

After the dog was fed and watered he went from room to room sniffing each corner and baseboard. "He'd better not do what I think he's going to do," Apolonia said, but when he found the newspapers in the bathroom and knew what they were for she agreed to give it a try for a week. "If I'm still alive and he hasn't destroyed the house," she added, "we'll try it for another week."

"What are you going to call him?" I asked.

"Honey, or Dear. Maybe if I beg and grovel and ingratiate myself to him he won't bite me."

"No," Mom said. "Call him Attila. Then if that guy comes around the house you can yell out, 'Attila, there's someone at the front door. Tie up the dog.' And he'll think Attila's your husband."

"The concept's good," Apolonia said. "But Attila? That's a little over the edge."

"Well, you want a strong male name, don't you?"

"How 'bout Gunther?" I asked.

"Or Otto?" Tony said.

"I had a boyfriend named Ted once," Apolonia said wistfully. The dog lifted its head, stood up, pattered over to her and lay down beside her chair. "He was my first boyfriend. Do you like the name Ted?" she asked the dog. He pushed himself up on its front paws and looked at her expectantly.

"Come 'ere, Ted," Tony said from across the room. The dog lifted itself up, crossed and stood in front of him, its tail wagging. It looked from Tony to Apolonia and back.

"Lay down, Ted," Apolonia said, pointing to the nest of blankets. The dog circled on the blanket several times and then lay down. "I think his name's Ted." The dog stood up, looking at Apolonia. "No, no, lay down, Ted." The dog, still looking at Apolonia, lay down and put his chin on his paws. "It's sort of like having a puppet with no strings," she said.

"Are you still afraid of him?" I asked.

"A little, but I think it's going to be okay."

"Between the sensor lights and the dog I know you're going to be okay," Mom said. "Any dog who doesn't like orthopedic shoes is okay in my book. I think you should call him Mr. Ted. Show a little respect."

The dog stood up, looking from Mom to Apolonia. Waiting. "Lay down, Ted," Apolonia said. "Go to sleep." The dog lay down, snorted and closed his eyes.

Fifty-One

Close to midnight Apolonia called and left a message on the answering machine. The sensor lights had gone on, and Ted had begun barking at something outside the living room window. "But it was only a cat in the bushes," Apolonia said. "I just thought you'd want to know."

Fifty-Two

The renovations at *Just for Tonight* were ahead of schedule and Maryanne began inviting us over for dinner. "Poulet au champagne again?" Tony teased her one night as we sampled one of the meals she planned to put on the menu when the restaurant opened in the spring. The dining room had five small tables with seating for four and a larger table that could seat eight. Our voices seemed to echo in the near empty room.

Mom punched him lightly on the arm and he pretended to ward her off with a crossed knife and fork.

"Would you rather have a peanut butter sandwich on rye?" Maryanne laughed.

When dinner was over and mom and I were helping her clear away the dishes Tony asked how soon she thought they would be able to start renting rooms.

"Our bedroom and the nursery are finished and four of the rooms on the second floor are almost ready. One of the smaller ones on the third floor is all set, too. Why?"

"I ran into a guy I knew when I was working in Boston. He's in a bind. His wife's on his back because he invited all his relatives from Maine to stay with them over Thanksgiving and now there's no room for her cousin Charlie and his wife and kids. I guess his wife can be a cross to bear if she doesn't get her way. Any chance you could put them up?"

"When would they be getting here?"

"They're driving up from Arizona and'll get here sometime in the afternoon the day before Thanksgiving. It would be just Charlie, his wife and their two teenaged sons. They're coming for the Indian Day of Mourning and I figured since Cole's Hill is right down the street from you that would really be convenient. What should I tell him?"

"Tell him that's fine as long as he understands that they're our first customers and we're just new at this." She stacked the dishes in the washer and asked, "What time should I plan dinner?"

"That won't be a problem. They fast until sundown and then they'll have dinner with some friends so you wouldn't have to worry about rushing to open the restaurant for anyone except us on Thanksgiving day."

Fifty-Three

The day before Thanksgiving was bitterly cold. My breath frosted in the air as I scraped a thin skim of ice off my windshield and whitecaps blew across the dark blue, almost black, waves in the harbor. The car finally warmed up as I drove into the parking lot at work. I left at noon because there was a possibility the Sagamore Bridge would be closed because of high winds and would have left me stranded at the nursing home. I searched the closets for extra sheets and pillows and brought them over to the bed and breakfast and began making up the beds. Frank's partner came back from the store with bags of vegetables and began stacking squash and turnips into the bin in the kitchen. When he saw that I was there and found out why he said, "How 'bout the other rooms? Could you rent them out? Dad's got a funeral for the day after Thanksgiving and there are ten people flying down from Alaska. He's been calling around but no luck so far. Could you put them up here?"

"If they're willing to rough it," Maryanne said. "Make sure they know we're not really open yet but two of the rooms have double beds and pullout sofas. Do we have enough sheets, mom."

"Sure," I said, "I'll make up the rooms in the attic."

She tipped the bin and picked through the squash and turnips, "You'd better get more of those and see if you can track down a couple more fresh turkeys."

"Where am I gonna find fresh turkeys the day before Thanksgiving?"

"I think I know where I can get an extra one," I said. It was the policy of our nursing home that all employees received a free Thanksgiving turkey. When I picked up mine I brought Maxine's back for her and left it in her office. She was vague when we talked about our plans for Thanksgiving and later Judy explained that Maxine had no family in the area and seemed to spend her holidays alone. "But it's a deep dark secret." Judy said, "She never lets anyone in on her personal life and if you try to invite her to join you she just locks down. Always says she has other plans but I don't believe her." When Maxine and I walked out together after work that night I asked her to join us but she said she had other plans.

While Maryanne mixed the bread dough I tried to reach Maxine on the phone. After three tries I finally got through. "Max," I said, "I feel like a sleaze asking you this, and I wouldn't, except that I'm desperate."

"Stop beatin' around the bush. Whadda yah need?"

"Your turkey. And I'm not going to be able to get away to pick it up. Would you mind bringing it here?"

"Where are yah?"

"I'm at Maryanne and Kevin's place. Can you do it? Please?"

"I'll try," she said. "Anything else yah want me to pick up on the way over? Like the Hope Diamond or sumpthin'?"

She arrived three hours later flushed and out of breath, cradling the turkey in her arms. Her car had stalled in the middle of a nearby parking lot and wouldn't start and while Tony went over to get it running again she rolled up her sleeves, put on an apron and joined Maryanne, the chef and myself in preparing for the next day's growing onslaught of guests. The mixing bowls and cutlery were put away and the counters had been scrubbed when Tony came back and announced that there was a problem with the distributor cap and that he had managed to get the car into a parking spot. Maryanne took off her apron and asked Kevin to put the folding cot up in the nursery because Maxine was staying over.

"Can't," Maxine said, "I've got other plans." Tony looked at his watch and then told her that the car wasn't going anywhere and that the chances of getting it fixed would be pretty slim since the repair involved finding a place that was open that had a distributor cap. "I've got other plans," Maxine said again, slipping into her coat and pulling her gloves out of the pockets.

Maryanne's eyes filled with tears and her chin trembled. "Maxine," she said, "Stay. You've got to help me. All of the sudden all these people are coming," her voice became shrill, "and I need all the help I can get. Everything's getting out of hand. Can't you call and cancel your plans?"

Maxine put her arm around Maryanne and hugged her, "Okay, okay," she said softly, "I'll try. Where's a phone?" I listened to the drone of her voice in the kitchen as Maryanne and Kevin bundled into coats and scarves and left for a walk on the waterfront.

"All set?" I asked Maxine when she came into the living room.

"They were a little upset but they'll get over it." She grunted, kicked off her shoes and sat down beside me on the sofa. While we arranged cloves in oranges and stacked them in the wicker basket in front of the gas stove the wind gusted against the windows and whistled around the corners of the house. "I never met a woman who needed a nap more than your daughter. You know what her problem is?" Maxine finally said.

"Who? Whose problem?"

"Your daughter's problem."

"I have no idea. Everything was going so well."

"That's my point. Everything's goin' too well. Faster than she thought and it scares her because she's afraid of success. You've got the same problem. You're wowin' 'em at work. The residents love yah. The families listen to yah. You're even getting' along with the nurses and you're still not sure of yourself, are yah?" I shrugged, "You still want your friend's job, don't yah?" When I didn't answer she asked me again, "Well? Don't yah?"

I shrugged again and didn't answer. When I went into the kitchen to make popcorn and hot chocolate I noticed Maxine had left the phone on the counter. I lifted it from the table and was about to put it back in its cradle then looked over my shoulder to make sure Maxine wasn't watching and pressed the redial button. I hoped I wouldn't recognize the voice of the person on the other end of the line. I was so engrossed in how I would respond if it turned out to be Judy or Mr. Montgomery that it took several minutes to realize I was listening to Dial-A-Prayer.

Maryanne and Kevin came home and settled down in the smaller front living room to watch television. The plane from Alaska was delayed by bad weather and Charlie and his family hadn't arrived yet but called from Connecticut to say cars were pulling off to the side of the road because of heavy snow squalls. "This was a great idea," Maxine said, "to have separate living rooms for kids and adults. And if kids try to escape from this room and book it out the front door they have to go through your office and you catch 'em. We should have somethin' like this for the wanderers at work. Why don't you go on home, Gloria," Maxine lifted her chin and tilted her head towards Maryanne who was pushing back her cuticles and tapping her foot on the floor. "I've got everything under control."

The walk home was bitterly cold. I blew on my mittened hands and pulled up the collar of my coat close around my ears for warmth as I hurried along the nearly deserted streets until a cluttered display in an antique shop caught my eye. An oval mirror in a carved oak frame was propped against an easel in the center of the display. I had been looking for a Christmas present for Maryanne and Kevin; something for the bed and breakfast and the mirror seemed perfect. The price tag was turned to the side and as I stooped to see if I could read it I saw my image and the reflection of the empty street behind me. I shrugged at my reflection as I thought over what Maxine had said. "'Well? Don't yah?'" I whispered softly, and realized that I honestly didn't know.

Fifty-Four

That night around ten, when Charlie and his family arrived, Maxine insisted on giving them a tour of the house. When the teenaged boys unloaded a large drum from the back of the van Maxine settled their parents on the second floor and showed them to a room in the attic. Around midnight the family from Alaska arrived and Maxine made them coffee and stayed with them until after two in the morning listening as they reminisced and shared faded photos of the eighty-five year old feisty woman who had been the matriarch of their large family.

In the morning Apolonia arrived before most of the guests were up. Maryanne insisted that she bring her dad's wheel chair into the kitchen and while she poured him a cup of coffee Apolonia went back outside to bring in the dog. When she undid Ted's leash he bounded through the house, his nails clattering on the floor, skidding on throw rugs and thudding against the walls. As he began to settle down he paced from room to room until we cornered him and barricaded him in the living room where he circled and curled into a tight ball in front of the gas log fireplace.

Maxine and Charlie's wife Inez helped arrange the tables in the large dining room. She told us that she and Charlie had met years ago on Thanksgiving Day when they had both marched from Cole's Hill after the memorial service to retrieve the bones of an Indian girl that had been unearthed when a road was being built. The bones of the unknown girl were taken to a museum where they remained until the day Inez met Charlie. "We marched down the street and I kept noticing this tall handsome guy from the corner of my eye. Once we got inside the museum they closed the doors and the drumming began. It echoed off the granite walls and I suddenly realized I was alone.

I didn't know anyone. Surrounded by strangers. Cops outside. Crowds inside. I could hardly breath. Then I backed into Charlie and he grinned and said, 'It's all right. I'm here,' and we've been together ever since."

"Why did ja go in the first place?" Maxine asked.

"Go where?"

"To the museum."

"Well, when I was a student at Mass Art I had a teacher who thought she was the reincarnation of Nephratiti. She had this long neck and regal bearing," Inez smoothed out a tablecloth and began laying out the silverware, "so of course that involved a lot of trips to the museum to check out her relatives. The mummies. But I always felt unclean after we left the museum. Like we were grave robbers or ghouls. People, no matter who they are, should be buried properly not put on display. Since I couldn't do anything about them I thought maybe I could do something for that little unknown girl."

Maxine rolled her eyes at me and said to Inez, "You shoulda been a social worker."

She turned and winked at me. "I am," she said.

Breakfast was a simple affair of cranberry juice, coffee and over sized warm walnut pumpkin muffins with honey butter. The family from Alaska insisted that Maxine join them. Before we began eating they joined hands and bowed their heads to say grace, including Maxine in their circle. Maxine reached out to Apolonia who reached out to mom who took Maryanne's hand, then mine.

After breakfast Apolonia folded her father's wheel chair and loaded it into the trunk of her car and we drove to Plymouth Plantation. The scuttling clouds were thick and gray and there was a crisp smell of snow in the air.

"I used to do this every Thanksgiving," I said. "After we put the turkey in the oven we'd bundle up the kids and come down here."

"Every year?" Apolonia said, unfolding her father's wheel chair and helping him into it. As she pushed her dad's chair over the bumpy, rutted road that led down the hill to the cluster of small, thatched roof houses she said, "Talk about memory loss! No wonder you're right at home with dementia patients."

"When they were little they thought it was an adventure. And afterwards on the way home, we'd stop on Cole's Hill. When the drumming and the prayers began there'd be a hush and you could feel a solemnness growing in the crowd. Even the kids calmed down and became quiet. Of course there were always these guys in the crowd who seemed a little out of place. Polyester suits and coats with sleeves a little too short. Their hats never seemed to fit. Tony swears that they were undercover FBI agents and that our pictures are on file somewhere."

"Do you still go?"

"No. Not for years," I said. When other groups began making it their day the day lost its focus as the Indians couldn't just show up adlib and instead had to arrive exactly at noon to be in front of the TV cameras and meet time schedules. The cables crisscrossing the ground seemed to leech the sacredness out of the earth beneath my feet. The expectant hush disappeared in the milling hubbub of a crowd caught up in festive protests and the Day of Mourning lost all meaning for me.

The light snow that had begun when we first got out of the car turned to flurries by the time we reached the first straw thatched house. Two men standing in the crowd outside smiled at Apolonia, lifted her father's wheelchair and carried it inside.

Apolonia smiled back, turned up the collar of her coat and

whispered, "I think the blond one's interested. Should we invite them back for dinner?"

"There's no room at the inn," I whispered back. "Besides, it's the guy with the green eyes and salt and pepper hair that's got his eye on you."

"Really?" Apolonia smiled again and they smiled back. They laughed and joked easily with Apolonia as they pushed the wheelchair down the sloping hill and around the frozen ruts in the path between the two rows of houses lifting the wheelchair in and out of the next three houses. But, by the time we reached the fourth house it was obvious they more interested in her father's interaction with the actors immersed in their Pilgrim personas than they were in Apolonia. Her father's confusion increased as the people he met seemed to be firmly locked into the 1600's and refused to step out of character and into his world when he talked to them. His agitation roiled to the breaking point when a plump, round faced woman insisted he looked like he was related to John Alden. She introduced herself as Priscilla Mullins and asked him if he would try to convince John that she was a good cook. "Lady, I don't know you and I don't know John Alden," he said, "and besides, how do I know you're a good cook?"

"Thee be right, How could thee know?" Priscilla Mullins said and broke off small pieces of drab gray bread. She passed one small lump to Apolonia's dad and another piece to a little girl who had been following the wheelchair from house to house and was leaning against it. The little girl was wearing a handmade birthday sign on her fake fur coat: *I'm Five Today.* Red mittens dangled from the ends of an elastic ribbon that ran up one sleeve, through the coat and down the other sleeve. Her mother kept snugging on her mittens and adjusting her white rabbit's fur hat. The bread was as hard as stone. Apolonia's father spit it on to the floor then said to the child beside him, "What the hell kind of shit is this!"

The little girl slowly raised her mittened hand and fished the piece of bread from her mouth. "Pfft, Pfft," she said, trying to spit out the wisps of red wool on her tongue. She frowned at the soggy gray mass, pulled off her glove and began picking more wisps of wool from her lips, "Shit," she said, and handed the bread to her mother. Her mother looked like she had just been gifted with a coiled snake.

"No, darling, it's bread," her mother said, looking around for a place to put it down. She waited until she thought no one was looking, then opened her hand and pretended it accidentally fell to the floor. She rubbed spittle and grit off the palm of her hand against her coat and grimaced.

"Shit," the little girl said again.

"Don't say that, darling. That's not nice."

Apolonia's dad looked up at the woman and said, "Why?" Then he looked at the little girl and said, "Shit's shit, kid, and don't you forget it."

"Shit," the little girl said. "Shit, shit, shit." Her mother grabbed the red mitten and reeled her out of the house on the end of the elastic ribbon.

By now the two men were helpless with laughter as Apolonia and I struggled to get the wheelchair through the narrow door way. "What's next?" her father grinned, squinting up at us through the blinding snow.

"Dinner," Apolonia grunted as she leaned her weight into the wheelchair and began pushing it up the hard uneven ground.

"That didn't take long," her father said.

"Long enough," she said grimly.

Fifty-Five

After dinner I rode back to Churchill Lakes with Apolonia. Her father dozed in the back seat while Ted, sitting beside him, pressed his nose against the slightly open window. Each time we talked Ted turned towards us expectantly, poking up one ear and then the other, as though listening to our conversation. "Dad's exhausted," Apolonia said, as we neared the nursing home, "Let me get him inside and then I'll drive you home."

"I'll help," I said. "Leave Ted in the car and the heater running." I slipped on a patch of snow-covered ice as I stepped out of the car and nearly fell into a deep drift. "On second thought," I said, "wait here and I'll go inside and get a nurse's aide to come out and help."

As soon as I stepped into the warmth of the dimly lit unit I felt an aura of tension. A resident, dressed for bed, sat in his wheelchair in the doorway of his darkened room and looked down the hallway at Ruby who was pacing behind the nurse's station. Two Haitian male aides were trying to calm her. Several residents sat across from the station and one, Lucy, prayed loudly in Italian while fingering plastic rosary beads. "What's up?" I asked.

"Marilyn saw my husband hiding in the bushes out back." Ruby's voice was brittle and she clenched and unclenched her fists. "We had a terrible fight before I left for work tonight," she said, "and now he's out there waiting for me to come off duty."

"Don't worry, Ruby," the taller aide said, his voice a deep comforting rumble, "We called the police. They'll be here soon." He put his arm around her and turned his head aside to whisper in my ear, "But the roads are so bad they're not here yet."

"Apolonia's out there with her dad," I whispered back.

"Stay here with Ruby," the other aide said, "We'll get them inside."

After they left Ruby tore a tissue from a box beside the phone and dabbed at her nose. She pushed the tears from her face with her fists and said, "Gloria, go down and see if Marilyn's heard anything more on the scanner."

The drapes were pulled and the lights were off in Marilyn's room. She was sitting in the dark beside the window and holding back an edge of the drape. As I tapped lightly on the door she put a finger against her lips and motioned me to the other side of the window. Each time the police scanner squawked to life in spurts of static Marilyn tilted her head and listened carefully.

"Where is he?" I asked.

She motioned me to her side and pulled the drape a little wider until we both had a clear view of the parking lot. All the cars in the lot, except for Apolonia's, were shrouded in snow. The taller aide struggled to keep his balance as he carried Apolonia's father in his arms towards the front door. The other braced himself against the wind that kept catching the wheelchair and pulling him around in circles. Ted struggled to wiggle his way out of the car and several times his hind legs slid out of the car and skittered on the trampled snow around the car until Apolonia finally managed to push him inside and slam the door. She looked back over her shoulder at the car and the moon lit snow covered bushes that lined the parking lot several times as she stumbled after the aides.

Marilyn pushed back the drape and with the heel of her hand cleared a swath through the condensation on the windowpane. "There he is!" she shouted. The snow gusted and swirled as a man bundled in a hooded parka that hid his face stepped from behind the bushes and up to Apolonia's car. He swung a baseball bat at the front window and then began to work his way systematically around the car smashing first one window and then the next until he had destroyed them all. He lifted the bat again and smashed out the headlights, ignoring Ted's muffled barking that almost blanketed the sound of sirens as police cars neared the building. Flickering strobes of red and blue lights pierced through the falling snow. Ted suddenly vaulted through the broken back window, skidded to the front of the car and lunged at the man's back nearly knocking him to the ground. When the man regained his balance he raised the bat above his head and swung his foot back. Ted, who seemed to crouch and cower at the man's feet suddenly, lunged forward again but this time the attack was low. He caught the man's trouser leg between his teeth and pulled back. During the struggle the man raised his foot and slammed the dog against the car. In the process he lost his footing and fell to the ground.

The first police car slid to a halt at the entrance to the nursing home and Marilyn screamed through the closed window, "Not there, you moron, here! *Here!*"

The man, on his feet again, pushed Ted away and scrambled into Apolonia's car. The car skidded forward thudding against several cars in the lot before side swiping a second police car that pulled into the driveway on its way to the back entrance. Both cars spun around twice before Apolonia's car, shrouded in a cloud of swirling snow, roared through the bushes and swerved across the shadowed lawn. Gathering momentum, the car skinned the bark from several hemlock trees then rammed into the massive beech tree at the entrance to the parking lot. Sparks rained into the darkness.

The night was suddenly very still except for the muffled blare of the car's horn.

A short stocky policeman, his arms held out from his sides,

lumbered slowly toward the car. The static on the police scanner cleared and we listened as his backup called for an ambulance.

Ruby rushed out of the building slipping and falling several times as she dashed towards the car. The policeman reached out and tried to hold her back but she pushed him away and ran into the woods as the car burst into flames. The police followed, the beam of their flashlights crisscrossing in the snow as they searched for the driver of the car.

"He escaped," Marilyn said softly, her eyes wide with fear. "Do you think he could get inside here?"

I shook my head no but reached out to make certain that the latches on her windows were secure.

Apolonia had come into the room and was standing beside me. "Poor Ruby," she said.

When Ruby finally came back inside I wrapped her in blankets while Apolonia rubbed her feet. "That bastard was thrown through the window," she said as she breathed on her fingers to warm them. "It looked like he broke his neck when he hit the ground."

"How awful for you, Ruby," Apolonia said, rocking her in her arms.

"How awful is right," Ruby said, "It wasn't Jack."

"Are you sure?" I asked.

"This guy was bald," she pulled the blanket closer as Apolonia sat back on her heels, "Jack's weird but he never had a devil's head tattooed on the back of his neck."

Apolonia reached up and squeezed my hand until it hurt.

Fifty-Six

I sat between Apolonia and Ted in the backseat of the cruiser and tried unsuccessfully calm them down as we drove to the station. The snow had turned to sleet and Apolonia cried out each time the car swerved on the icy roads. I tried to calm myself by focusing on the steady strum of the windshield wipers as they knifed across the front window cracking the thin veneer of ice and pushing it away. When the rubber on one wiper came loose and the windshield arm began to scrape across the glass Ted whimpered and moaned and then struggled to crawl over my lap to get to Apolonia. I held his collar fast and he pressed his nose against the side window and clawed frantically at the door beside him. The driver's eyes narrowed as he looked back at us in the rearview mirror.

When we finally got to the station the driver, who introduced himself as Sergeant Williams, showed us in to a small spartan room off the main lobby. He settled us into chairs across the desk from himself. He and Apolonia began filling out a restraining order while Ted paced in tight figure eights in the corner of the room, occasionally casting suspicious looks over his shoulder in their direction. I called Tony and explained what had happened and asked him to come pick us up.

While we waited in the cramped room, sipping mugs of steaming coffee, I asked Apolonia why she needed a restraining order. "It looks like he's paralyzed from the neck down," I said, "it's not like he's not going anywhere."

Apolonia suddenly slammed her hand down against the table with such force that coffee splashed over the rim of the thick mug and onto the desk. Sergeant Williams whipped a handkerchief from his trouser pocket and leaned across the table to clean up the spill. His eyes never left Apolonia. "Just listen to *me*," she shouted at him, "Do you hear me?"

"I hear you," he said calmly but he glanced nervously towards the empty lobby as he slid the mugs closer to me and sat back down. I thought he was being cautious and was trying to prevent Apolonia from using the scalding coffee as a weapon until I realized his edginess was due to a sin of compassion when I noticed a neatly printed sign on the wall behind him: No food or beverages are to be brought into this room.

"Don't listen to *her*. Just, just," Apolonia waved her hand then ran her fingers through her hair. I reached out and tried to hold her hand but she pulled away. *"'Looks'* like he can't go anywhere," she hissed at me, "You don't know him, Gloria. I do. I'm not taking chances." She leaned across the table towards Sergeant Williams and her voice became a low growl, "I have never in my entire life wished anyone dead but…" Sergeant Williams raised an eyebrow and glanced in my direction. I shook my head, no. Ted shifted from paw to paw. Sat down. Stood up. Ducked his head and began to pace again. Apolonia began to sob and pulled her coat tighter around her body. "You're never too old to learn new tricks, are you Ted?" she said bitterly. The dog hearing his name crouched low and crossed the room slowly. She reached down, wrestled him onto her lap and his pink tongue began licking the salty tears from her face.

"M'am, do you have any firearms in your house?" the Sergeant asked her while looking at me. Again I shook my head, no.

"Of course not," Apolonia shouted. "Are you nuts? Do you think I'd be in this fix if I **had** a *firearm?*" She wrapped her arms around Ted and buried her face against his neck.

Fifty-Seven

Christmas was usually a hectic season at our house but now that Maryanne had a home of her own and Bradley had called to say he was spending the holidays in California with his roommate and their friends Christmas decorations or the scent of pine couldn't fill the empty places in my heart. I felt that time had truly turned back in its flight and made me a child again but by some pitiless quirk had stopped short at the year when I first experienced the total loss of knowing there was, without a doubt, no Santa Claus. Even the Coca Cola commercial brought tears to my eyes. Christmas carols left me bereft. Especially on the night Tony, Mom and I settled down in the living room to watch *Frosty the Snowman* together. When that cartoon ended and before *Yogi's First Christmas* came on I went out to the kitchen to bring in a plate of Christmas cookies and a pitcher of milk. On my way through the darkened dining room I head mom say to Tony, "I can't take too much more of this."

"Humor her, mom, she's having a tough time," Tony said.

"This is the third cartoon tonight. How many more do we have to watch?"

"We used to do this when the kids were little. Cheer up. Christmas is nearly over. Just three more weeks to go and life'll get back to normal."

Mom groaned, "I don't think I can last that long." She raised her voice and called out, "Gloria? While you're out there could you get me a Tums?" I backed through the dining room into the kitchen so they wouldn't catch me crying,

Fifty-Eight

I expected the sudden waves of sadness that washed over me at unexpected times when I was home to overwhelm me at work but surprisingly, as small artificial trees and wreathes began to decorate the resident's rooms the first joyous seeds of Christmas were replanted and began to blossom in my heart.

The maintenance men, a tall lanky blond referred to as the 'Marlboro Man' and his sidekick, a short balding brunette with horn rimmed glasses and an off beat sense of humor, always showed up together whether they were asked to wallpaper a room or replace a light bulb. Together they set up dark green wooden shelves in a corner of the foyer. The shelves tapered upwards towards the ceiling in the shape of a Christmas tree and the following morning staff and visitors began bringing in poinsettia plants and arranging them on the shelves. After a hurried call to the medical director the maintenance team was back to set up a low white fence around the base of the tree to prevent Minnie, a recently admitted pleasantly confused wanderer from eating the bright red leaves.

In the afternoon Kathleen and the volunteers who had gradually returned once Paul was discharged, laced wires of small white lights through the plants. In the evening the lobby lights were dimmed and the receptionist put a CD of Christmas carols on the stereo.

Each evening before the long ride home I began to sit with the residents who lounged on the sofas or in the wing backed chairs enjoying the beauty of the tree while they waited for dinner to be served. Gradually the vague feeling of emptiness drained away and was replaced with a sense of peace and contentment.

On the night of the tree lighting in Shirley Square I

suggested that mom and Tony walk downtown with me.

"But the *Winnie the Pooh Christmas* special is on," Tony said. Mom winced and stepped behind my back. I knew she was waving her arms at him and probably glaring and drawing her finger across her throat.

Vendors were setting up their carts and the smell of roasting chestnuts and hot pretzels mingled with the scent of pine as we neared the blocked off Square. Groups of caroling school children moved through a crowd that had begun to gather near a fold up metal table where Boy Scouts were selling hot chocolate and donuts. The heavy lower boughs of the Christmas tree swayed as the wind swept up North Street and sighed through their full branches. The lower arms of the two stories high tree held in place by guy wires, spread from the edge of one of the brick buildings over the curb and spilled into the street. The dark branches were wreathed in curled bands of golden ribbon and red velvet bows.

I spotted Maryanne and Kevin standing near a cluster of Victorian carolers who had gathered in the street in front of one of the decorated historic homes that had opened their doors for tours and cinnamon spiced cider.

"Now that's just plain foolish," Mom said as we started down the street towards them, "putting candles inside paper bags on the side of the road like that with all these children around."

"They're luminaries, mom," I said.

"I don't care what they are they're dangerous." Her breath was coming in short gasps.

"Are you alright?" I asked.

"I'm fine," she said, loosening her scarf and holding it in front of her nose and mouth.

"No you're not. You're breathless."

"I'm cold." She nodded towards the small teashop we were passing and said, "I'm going in there for a few minutes to warm up. You go on ahead and I'll catch up with you later."

"Are you sure you're all right?"

"I'm all right," she said, waving me away.

"Do you think she's all right?" I asked Tony once we were alone.

"I don't know. We'll keep an eye on her. I noticed she was breathless the other night, too."

"Why didn't you say something then?"

"And piss off your mom? I don't think so."

Down by the waterfront the high school band fell into step behind the drone of a bagpiper and the parade up the hill towards the square began. Bringing up the end of the parade was a horse drawn open carriage driven by a stooped shouldered elderly man. Wisps of white hair poked out from beneath his top hat as he clucked from the corner of his mouth and slapped the reins against the prancing horse's back. Small children either cowered back against their parents or went wild with excitement when they saw that Santa and his wife were seated in the back of the carriage. The horse, who pulled the carriage through waterfront traffic in the heat of summer, oblivious to fire engines and roaring motorcycles, suddenly reared up when a group of children began shouting, "SanTA, SanTA," and the crowd picked up the chant. The horse's eyes widened and rolled from side-to-side and his ears twitched back flat against his head as the driver pulled the reins taut and regained enough control to bring the cart to an unsteady halt. Arms reached up and half led, half pulled Santa and his wife from the back of the cart. While she adjusted her clothes and patted her hair the old man in the top hat cursed and swore as the cart disappeared down the main street, around the barriers and into the night.

By the time we found mom and the ceremonial switch had been pulled to light the Christmas tree and the lights on the trees nearby, mom's breathing had returned to normal.

When we got home I put on a pot of coffee while mom changed into her nightgown and bathrobe. She came into the kitchen humming and then began singing *I Heard The Bells On Christmas Day*. "Remember that one, Gloria?" she said, sitting down at the table. "Tony, we had a tradition when she was a child. She and her brother would stand at the piano and sing while I played Christmas carols. It was the last thing they did before going to bed on Christmas Eve."

"Are you sorry you gave the piano away?" Tony asked.

"Sometimes," she said. Her voice trembled when she began to sing *Oh Little Town of Bethlehem* but grew stronger as Tony and I joined in. She spooned sugar into her coffee and stirred it thoughtfully. "On Christmas morning I'd be the first one awake. I'd go downstairs, light the tree, put on the coffee and then sit down and play carols to wake them up. She and Bradley would rush down the stairs in their pajamas...."

"Mom, we were always awake long before you."

"I know," she said, "but I didn't want to get up a three in the morning."

Fifty-Nine

As Christmas grew closer my visits with the residents became bitter sweet as some adjusted to the reality they would not be going home for the day and others verbalized their feelings as they counted a litany of losses. During the day carolers from the local schools and churches strolled through the building or gathered around the tree in the foyer. On the days when caroling was scheduled for the activities room I brought mom into work and she accompanied them on the piano. Afterwards, while I arranged transportation for those residents who would be spending the day with their families mom either visited with Maxine or stretched out on the sofa in my office and napped.

Maryanne, Kevin, and Frank and his partner volunteered to cater Christmas dinner at Churchill Lakes so the kitchen and dining room staff could spend the day with their families.

On the Friday before Christmas I was working later than usual. Maxine had finished signing in a new resident and was heading downstairs to her office when she noticed I was sitting behind the nurse's station. "Workin' late?" she asked, "On a weekend?"

"Finishing up," I said. "Would you mind waking up mom when you go down. Ask her to bring up my coat and pocketbook and close the office."

"Done," Maxine said.

I closed the chart I was working on and put it back in the rack. When I turned around Lucy's son was standing at the desk with a platter of thin, crisp Italian cookies. "A gift for the staff," he said, "For putting up with the Old Bat." As we talked I noticed Maxine scoop a blood pressure cuff off the medicine cart and motion to Ruby. The next time I looked over they were gone and Marilyn was maneuvering her wheelchair behind the nurse's station as a code blue was announced on the overhead page. Marilyn reached out and held my hand tightly.

"It's going to be all right," she said softly. "You're going to be all right."

"What happened?" Lucy's son asked.

"Maxine called 911. I heard it over the scanner. Gloria, your mom went into cardiac arrest."

Sixty

Bradley arrived in time to be a pallbearer at the funeral. The night before his flight back to California he, Maryanne and Kevin walked over to Simon's for dinner. They invited Tony and me to join them but instead, we spent the first part of the evening sitting quietly together in mom's room. He seemed almost relieved when Apolonia rang the doorbell later that evening. "I wanted to stop by for just a minute," she said. "I wanted to drop something off for Gloria."

Tony showed her into the room and she held me close for a moment then lit the five scented candles mom had arranged near the small créche on top of her dresser. Apolonia plugged in the plastic candle on the windowsill.

"What's this?" she asked, picking up one of the white stones mother kept there.

"A lucky stone," I said. "She must have had it with her when she had the run in with the alligator." My laughter erupted in short shuddering gasps.

Apolonia turned off the overhead light and came to sit on the edge of the bed beside me, "How are you doing?" she asked, putting her arm around my shoulder.

"Not too good," I said, resting my head on her shoulder.

"At least she died in her sleep. That's how I'd want to go," she said, "Wouldn't you?"

I nodded. She reached into the pocket of her sweater and took out a small box wrapped in silver foil and tied with coils of golden ribbon. "What's that?" I asked.

She passed the box to me, "Open it," she said.

I slowly untied the ribbons, opened the box and unfolded the iridescent tissue paper that nested Apolonia's Department of Social Services identification badge.

"It's yours," Apolonia said. "You always knew this job wasn't right for me. It just took me a little longer to figure it out."

"Are you sure you want to do this?" I asked.

"Absolutely. If you still want the job it's yours. I'll recommend you but you've got to help me write my resignation letter." When I tried to give her badge back she folded her hand over mine and said, "Don't make up your mind tonight. Think it over. Sleep on it. But," she gave me a quick hug, "In the meantime I'm serious about writing that letter."

"Are you sure?" I asked.

"Got any paper?" I handed her the box of floral stationary mother always kept on the nightstand next to her bed and she reached into her pocket again and took out a pen. "I'll need a stamp," she said, "Do you have any?"

I dug through coins and lint covered cough drops in the bottom of my shoulder bag until I found a book of stamps. I was about to throw out the cough drops and the small folded paper stuck to them when I realized it was Peter Michael's address. I left Apolonia alone in mom's room to write her letter and went into the kitchen. I slid the last packet of microwave popcorn from its box and stuffed the box with the funny papers from the Sunday Globe. Then I folded the lucky stone into the iridescent tissue, tucked it into the newspapers, wrapped the box and scrawled on Peter Michael's address.

Tony came into the kitchen, saw the popcorn on the counter and nuked it. "*The Christmas Carol's* on," he said. "It's the cartoon." I followed him into the living room and sat down on the sofa beside him, leaning into the protective curl of his arm and dipping my hand into the bowl of popcorn on his lap. He flicked on the cartoon and we put our feet up on the hassock to watch.

Apolonia finished her letter and came into the living room

to return the stamps. "Need anything mailed?" she said. "I'm going to swing by a mail box on my way home tonight."

"How many stamps do you think this would take?" I asked, handing the packaged lucky stone to Tony.

He hefted the small package in his hand and said, "Four. Maybe five stamps."

I put the rest of the stamps on the package, all twelve just in case, and gave the package to Apolonia. "Don't bother to get up," she said, "I'll let myself out."

The front door closed softly and Tony reached out and turned off the lap beside the sofa. The soft flickering light from the television set cast shadows across his face and I ran my finger along the lines etched around the corners of his mouth. "What?" he said, turning to look at me.

"Nothing," I said, "I was just thinking how lucky I was to have you in my life."

I stretched out on the couch and he pulled my feet onto his lap and massaged them absentmindedly. "The tree looks nice this year," he said. I looked across the room at the lighted tree and the ornaments we had collected over the years as the children grew up and we grew older. "I wish mom could be here to see how beautiful the tree looks tonight," I said.

"She's here," he said, "She knows."

"Do you feel her presence, too?" I asked.

He pointed the wand at the TV. and pretended to wrestle with an invisible force as he clicked from channel to channel, "Yes! *Yes*! She's *here*!" he said, "I can't get the damn cartoon back on!"

Sixty-One

I had the dream again last night.

A massive white bear with four solid paws lumbered slowly over a vast expanse of crystal ice towards mother. She stands alone on a vast sea of ice the color of her china blue eyes. Her short thick white hair and soft white flannel nightgown billow gently around her body like a drift of snow. She seems aware but unconcerned that the shambling bear is looming larger and larger on the horizon. Maryanne is not at my side this time but I'm not afraid. I feel comforted by a presence behind me as mother kneels down and holds out her arms. I'm about to step onto the ice to join her but she holds out her hand, palm up, and with a smile shakes her head no. Instead, I feel released as a little blond haired boy runs out from behind me and dashes into her arms.

The bear lies down on the ice, tucks its paws beneath its chest, stretches out its long neck against the ice, and appears to be instantly asleep while mother gathers the blond haired child into her arms. She turns and, together, they crawl onto the back of the sleeping bear, wrap their arms around each other and close their eyes.

I woke up this morning to a feeling of soft melancholy because I knew I would never have the dream again.

In the afternoon I called Apolonia to wish her a Merry Christmas, "and Apolonia," I said, "I slept on it."

"And?"

"And I'm not going to take the job. The Dalai Lama was right."

"How so?"

"'Sometimes not getting what you want is a wonderful stroke of luck.'"